# TO THE LAST CITY

# To The Last City

## Colin Thubron

Chatto & Windus
LONDON

Published by Chatto & Windus 2002

2 4 6 8 10 9 7 5 3 1

Copyright © Colin Thubron 2002

Colin Thubron has asserted his right under the Copyright, Designs
and Patents Act 1988 to be identified as the author of this work

First published in Great Britain in 2002 by
Chatto & Windus
Random House, 20 Vauxhall Bridge Road,
London SW1V 2SA

Random House Australia (Pty) Limited
20 Alfred Street, Milsons Point, Sydney,
New South Wales 2061, Australia

Random House New Zealand Limited
18 Poland Road, Glenfield,
Auckland 10, New Zealand

Random House (Pty) Limited
Endulini, 5A Jubilee Road, Parktown 2193, South Africa

The Random House Group Limited Reg. No. 954009
www.randomhouse.co.uk

A CIP catalogue record for this book
is available from the British Library

ISBN 0 7011 7362 9

Papers used by Random House are natural,
recyclable products made from wood grown in sustainable forests;
the manufacturing processes conform to the environmental
regulations of the country of origin

Typeset by Deltatype Ltd, Birkenhead, Wirral
Printed and bound in Great Britain by
Biddles Ltd, Guildford and King's Lynn

For Austin and Page

# Acknowledgements

I am grateful to John Hemming for permission to use his translations from Spanish chroniclers in *The Conquest of the Incas*; to Marisol Mosquera and Fernando Silva for vital help in Peru; and to the peace of the Santa Maddalena Foundation.

# One

As THEY descended towards the ravine, the mountains rose to meet them. They were entering a solitude deeper than any they had imagined. They felt themselves dropping out of the light. The cloud forest thinned, and gusts of warm air blew up from below. Their horses' hooves sent stones whistling into the chasm. Above them, the palisade of snow-peaks – the destination they could not imagine – was slung across half the sky.

All afternoon, along a barely traceable path, they corkscrewed five thousand feet down the ravine. The sun shone gently on them – it was Peru's winter – and there was no wind. Beneath them, the Apurimac river, depleted by the dry summer, still surged over its boulders. Ahead of them, as they dropped deeper – some on foot, some on horseback – the peaks of Vilcabamba were at last obliterated by the valley wall, which was split by vertiginous spurs and clefts.

The Belgian's thighs ached under the short, descending steps of his horse, and the Englishman's feet, by the fourth hour of walking, had worked loose and inflamed in their boots. But for the moment he was too engrossed to care, while in front of him the delicate priest went with an expression of exalted reverie which the others found ridiculous, but imagined they understood. Here and there a tense glitter of streams ran in the defiles, and whenever they crossed one they entered a tangle of wild fuchsias and trees clotted with moss and bromeliads.

At last the noise of the river rose out of the silence, and the trees filled with the pipe and squeak of unseen birds. The horses minced over a cable footbridge. On the far bank the muleteers had set up camp on a few square yards of level ground, and their numbers – five men with nine pack animals, and a cook – belonged to another century. Quechua natives – showing the recessed brows and chins of their Inca ancestors – they had been born to this wilderness. With their loose gait and mountaineers' lungs they had glided soundlessly down the valleyside. In the dusk they had turned loose the mules and now squatted among the baggage and harness, smoking and speaking a soft, guttural tongue. After they had set up the dining tent, they never entered it. Instead the Europeans and the *mestizo* guide squeezed inside on aluminium chairs around an aluminium table, while the cook crouched in the entrance pumping Calor gas into a rusty ring.

At first they sat with the awkwardness of strangers thrown together. But the darkness outside, and a sense of their isolation, turned them slowly convivial, grateful for one another. A vague excitement brewed up. They toasted their journey in cheap Chilean wine.

The guide, perched between the priest and the quiet Englishwoman, attempted a speech of welcome; but he felt a tinge of unease. These people understood nothing of this land. Their baggage included chocolates and cosmetics and cellular phones. Didn't they realise that the stars appearing above them were different? Only Louis, the obese Belgian, seemed expansive enough for the guide to risk a question. The man was rubbing his thighs with little grunts of disgust, and murmuring: 'We should have brought a litter!'

'A litter? What is that?' Then the guide asked: 'Are you sorry to be here?'

'Sorry?' The Belgian laughed: a rich, self-mocking sound. 'I didn't have a choice! My wife wanted to ride. She likes mountains and jungle.' He reached across to her hand. She smiled vacantly. He said: 'I'm a fool.'

But he did not look a fool. His eyes bulged heavy in a watchful face. Josiane might have been thirty years younger, it was hard to tell. She was pretty and delicate. The Englishman, staring across at Louis, guessed it was his second or third marriage. Josiane, in this confusing candlelight, looked half as real as he did.

She said: '*Louis fait seulement ce qu'il a envie de faire.*'

She seemed to speak only French, and the guide's misgiving deepened. The common factor among these people, the travel agent said, was that they spoke English. Again he thought he should say something: something between a welcome and a caution. He hunted for the words. 'You know this journey is not usual. I think that is why you have chosen it.' But he did not know. 'Over two hundred kilometres in fifteen days would not be so much but . . . but we are going through the heart of the eastern Andes. This is very hard country . . . We may be going for eight or nine hours a day. There are no level places. The *arrieros* will set up camp where they can.' They were listening now, but it wouldn't make any difference, he knew. Foreigners travelled in this country ignorant of its dangers and sanctities. Perhaps that was what protected them. He went on: 'Tomorrow night we will come to the Inca ruins of Choquequirau. Few people have reached them before, and nobody knows why this city was built. It is without history.'

'There must be memories,' the Englishman broke in. 'Aren't there stories?' He had pale eyes in a mobile face, rather handsome. But the guide felt a surge of instinctive dislike. Some nervous impatience set the Englishman's jaw quivering. He burnt with enthusiasm or intolerance at whatever anybody else was saying. 'What do local people think?'

'There are no local people. This land is empty.' The guide went on harshly: 'For six days we cross the Cordillera Vilcabamba. We'll reach the snowline at a 15,000-foot pass before descending. In the end we go into rain forest at Espiritu Pampa. Then we come to Vilcabamba.'

Perhaps he only imagined the group let out a faint, collective sigh. Vilcabamba. That, in the end, was what had lured them. These people were like children, in a way. He had been to Vilcabamba once before, and there was nothing there. Just stones sunk in the jungle. The Inca had laid them five hundred years ago as their last refuge against the Spaniards. What could they mean to these foreigners? Why did they come? It was not a good place, Espiritu Pampa. Its soil was bitter. The Spaniards had sacked it in the end, and the forest covered it over. People said the place was not at peace.

THE ENGLISHMAN lay in his sleeping-bag, listening to the

4

quick, regular breathing of his wife. In the faint light he could see that she had placed her boots between them, with her anorak and a water bottle. He knew she was awake because her breathing was audible. In sleep she was silent. He could feel her resentment like a vapour in the tent, and listened instead to the violence of the river over its boulders and to the double note of a night-bird somewhere.

Suddenly she said: 'Robert? What do you think of these people?'

She had not turned round.

He said: 'I might like the Belgian. He's a cynic, but he's intelligent. As for the priest – what's his name? Francisco? – it's impossible to know, since he hardly speaks. I think we can trust the guide; and the muleteers too. These fellows may look frail, but they must be made of iron.'

A tiny gap had opened where Josiane was. Because he did not know what he thought of her.

'The Belgian woman,' he said eventually, 'I thought she was his daughter at first. What do you guess she is? An actress? A dancer?'

Camilla only said: 'It's odd to see a man like Louis besotted.'

Then she went quiet, and the too-quick breathing resumed. Again he felt her resentment, her recoil from this whole journey. She was here in this wilderness, with these discordant people, because of him. She had never enjoyed people in the same way he did. She always wanted to appropriate them. Her friendships were narrow and steadfast. They bored him, accused him a little. They were too heavy, too exclusive.

It was he, in the end, who slept; but he awoke an hour

later to a vision of leaf-shadows printed by moonlight on the tent roof. He gazed up at them in astonishment. They looked starkly delicate: a jungle distilled across the canvas. Outside, the river seemed to be roaring through a deeper loneliness. Camilla was asleep, and this, for the moment, was all there was in the world: the forest stencilled over the moonlit tent, and the noise of the great river pouring through darkness towards the Amazon. The air had cooled. He felt a disembodied elation. It was recognisable from adolescence, and he heard himself breathing out, as he might have twenty years ago: *So I have lived, I have lived!*

CAMILLA HEARD him unzip the mosquito net in the entrance and go out. She had sensed something in her sleep, as if Robert were too big for the tent, and now that he had left it the air was quiet again, and cold. She looked up to see the same leaf pattern over the ceiling, and it made her afraid. The light was too chill and wan. She tightened the sleeping-bag round her neck. And who were these people they would never see again? The Belgian never focused her; she did not exist for him, not as a woman. Such things no longer mattered to her, she thought, or only a little. But she could never warm to him. And his wife, with her elf-locks and childish mannerisms, was already irritating. As for the priest Francisco, he looked at her with the nervous gaze of a deer, and never uttered. All this was fine for Robert, just as theatre was fine. Impermanence didn't trouble him. He pillaged people for their brains, their looks, their eccentricities, then moved on.

She had once loved his journey from obsession to obsession, and sometimes, nostalgically, still did. Seventeen years ago (could it be?) when they were first married, he had been impassioned by Ottoman architecture, then by minority religions in the Middle East, then by the survival of Aramaic, and had poured out articles which seemed touched by a cranky brilliance. While filing news items as a correspondent in Damascus, he had toured Syria with her in a frenzy of euphoria and frustration. She wondered about this energy now. For another fifteen years she had watched him shift from newspaper to newspaper, chafing at foreign editors' desks in London, always a bit too maverick to hold. People seemed to expect something important of him: a major editorship, a resounding book. Meanwhile his obsessions never died of their own accord; each was subsumed by the next one, then abandoned. Sometimes she felt that she too, at some unspecified time, had been left behind.

She closed her eyes against the tent ceiling. She did not care for mountains. She wasn't sure how fit she was. Alone in the tent, she despised herself for being here. She had always fallen in with Robert's passions instead of following her own. But her own lay smothered somewhere under the luxuriant growth of his. Her love of research – which the birth of a delicate son had reduced to a part-time profession – was different from Robert's: not a reworking or transformation of knowledge, but a passive pleasure in it. She sometimes wondered who she would have become if she had not married young. But probably the same, she guessed, almost the same. She imagined Robert standing outside in the night, dreaming of the Inca. Occasionally she sensed him on the verge of bitterness, as if he feared time was running away from him – and she felt a pin-prick of alarm.

OUTSIDE, UNDER that hallucinatory sky, Robert was astonished to see no moon at all. It was starlight only that had turned their tent into a shadow play. He had never seen such a sky. It was ablaze from end to end. As he gazed down on the river, he found himself smiling, as if drugged. Fireflies flickered among the shrubs where madonna lilies grew, and there were glow-worms in the grass. Above him the unfamiliar constellations glowed fuller and more intense than those of the northern hemisphere, so that the Milky Way was less a trickle of sparks than a white dust glittering solid from one horizon to the other. No wonder the Inca worshipped it.

He reached through the tent flap and pulled out his telescope and compass. The tiny needle was clearly visible in the starlight. It swung towards the black mass above them where their track climbed precipitously north. Beyond, he imagined the last cones and spires of the Andes erupting in an ice-tipped wall, then foothills descending into forest and the Amazon delta. It was there, where the mountains eased into jungle, that the Inca had built the last city of their once-vast empire. Vilcabamba: he loved the sound of the name. For a few years, at least, it had haunted both Spaniards and natives with the dream of the Inca return.

He rooted the tripod of his telescope among rocks, and edged its barrel up. It was not powerful – little more than a toy – but in its lens the Southern Cross flashed like a warning, and the dust of the Milky Way separated like shattered glass.

When Robert detached his gaze from the eyepiece, he had the illusion that the sky was pressing close above him, close on the whole earth. He rubbed his eyes to cleanse them. He was puzzled that under this intricate web of light the Inca, who believed themselves Children of the Sun, had known so little about the skies. They had no true astronomical calendar as the Aztec and Maya had. To them the stars were sacred animals which interacted with the earth: Orion became a llama which crossed the sky to drink from the Pacific.

These absences in culture fascinated him: they suggested not paucity, but something later generations had not understood. The Inca were pervaded by such enigmas. Their empire was contemporary with the European Renaissance, yet they seemed cocooned in a remote antiquity. And into this world the Spaniards had arrived like a brutal modern fact. Shod in steel, the conquistadors rode chargers and fired muskets. The Indians were armoured in gold and feathers. They were dispelled like a mist. A mere 170 Spaniards put to flight armies of tens of thousands, and within ten years the Inca empire vanished. It was as if a delicate picture had been exposed to sunlight and blanched instantly away.

To Robert, who had expended all his adult life on words, the knowledge that the Inca had never practised writing, had known no alphabet, intensified their mystery. Their memorial lay in half-interpreted ruins, and in their Quechua descendants who still walked these mountains in mournful amnesia. Robert had studied them in libraries until they became a nagging obsession. In Lima he had scrutinised their artefacts in museums, but only felt their distance increase. Their vestments woven with golden scales like those of some fantastical fish, their masks and flutes and ceremonial oar-blades, the regalia which splashed gold down half their bodies – all seemed charged with some impenetrable symbolism.

Could it be true that they had never known writing? If so, theirs would be almost unique among great empires. Robert could not resist the idea that Western eyes, including his own, had been blind to something extraordinary, and that the gap left by script had been filled by some other, lost idiom – by a language free from the concepts an alphabet embodied: a language encoded in music, perhaps, or in the hieroglyphs of fabrics, even in the patterns of stars or the intricate layout of Inca cities. The need to inscribe meanings, finding no outlet in words, had expressed itself – he was quite sure – somewhere else.

He heard a baritone voice behind him. 'A different sky, isn't it? Can't locate a thing.' Louis was standing a yard away. 'The first telescope, you know – Galileo's, I think it was – showed the stars *square* and *rectangular*. Pretty upsetting, in its way.' He looked outlandishly comfortable in the chill night, his double chin nestled in the neck of silk pyjamas. 'Square stars didn't conform to expectation, of course, so people redeveloped the telescope. They didn't want anything angular flying about up there.'

Robert thought he could like Louis. He said: 'I dare say the Inca saw them square. They never did invent the wheel.' He noticed the white curve of Louis's stomach overlapping his pyjamas, and wondered vaguely about Josiane. How could she bear him on her? He pointed to the telescope. 'Do you want to take a look?'

The Belgian shrugged. 'I can see enough from here. Too much, in fact. Hurts the eyes.'

'It's astonishing.'

'Yes, well, this mountain stratosphere. There's less

carbon dioxide, of course; leaves the place pure.' He glanced up. 'But God, what a mess up there! Wreckage floating about in its own slipstream. And people talk about the order of the heavens. Gravitational pull – just a lottery! It makes you sick to look at it.' He roared his rich laughter. Then suddenly: 'You're a journalist, aren't you?'

'I was,' Robert said. 'I quit my paper to travel here.'

'Quit?' Louis looked suspicious.

'I turned freelance. Quite a risk, in its way. But how long do you wait?'

'Wait for what?' Louis was scratching his stomach.

Robert hesitated. It was a little humiliating to explain: how you harboured an ambition like a caged animal. For years the animal barely stirred. He had even thought it dead. Then it started pacing again: the desire to do the thing before it became too late and the animal died, smelling of rancour. But one morning he had decided to release it: the passion to write something different. To give voice to however the Inca had left behind the memory of themselves, as he travelled this once-sacred land. To write it before journalism coated all the words. Before he became afraid to put to the test his instinct that the Inca might have found some unsuspected language.

But it sounded too naive to talk about now. Because probably only he believed that this cipher might survive – in stone or pottery decoration or the configuration of ruins – or that the potential for sensing it existed in him, that it wasn't just a feeling. Not a capacity at all – he could imagine Louis scoffing – just the floating conviction of one: a booby trap. So when he said to Louis 'I mean to write about this journey,' he felt frailty beating up inside him like a warning.

11

Louis said: 'To write what?'

'A book, a slim book.'

'Well then, do it, Monsieur, do it! Get it out of your system.' But the Belgian shook his head slightly. He had straw-coloured curls which looked faintly dissolute. 'When I was a young architect I longed to design a country villa, but nobody gave me the commission. Ours was a very urban practice, in Hainaut. So I bought a plot and built the villa myself. An imitation Frank Lloyd Wright. Sold it for a pittance!' He laughed, a little cruelly. 'But I see now the villa was a fake. Whenever I drive past it, I take my glasses off. Hah–hah–hah!'

Robert felt too piqued to join the laughter at this warning. He said: 'Well, I'm not as young as you were then.' He folded up the telescope. 'All the same, look at this country! If anything can cleanse your eyes, it's this!'

He realised he sounded foolish, but it was too late.

Louis had burst into laughter again. It was a rolling, guttural sound, now not unkind. 'Ah. The cleansed eye! Self-obliteration. You are very ambitious.'

'Yes.' And Robert remembered other charges. You are self-centred: yes. Arrogant: probably. Overbearing: yes (she says so). All these things. Yes.

'But why Vilcabamba, Monsieur? Why not London, if you want a challenge. It would be harder to write about home.'

Robert said: 'Because Vilcabamba was the Incas' last memory of themselves. It was their last effort to perpetuate themselves.'

He thought: there, if anywhere, they must have longed to shore up their past, the history which they could not hold in writing, as their empire faded away. The desire to

12

commemorate must have been unbearable. To travel here, he thought, would be a kind of pilgrimage. For once he would set out with no journalistic motive, hunt no specific story, impose no opinion. He didn't know how it would end. He just trusted it. And he trusted himself. It was a great arrogance. He had never felt so elated. He looked at the precarious line of their camp above the river – a light still glimmered in the priest's tent – and at their mules and horses huddled beyond. He did not want to talk about himself any more. 'And you, Louis? You desert your architectural practice for this folly.'

'Ah no, my practice deserted me. I was made redundant – at fifty-six! People fell out of love with my buildings. They decided they were post-modern and that, in provincial Belgium, is the end. They thought me inept when I was only playful.' His feet made a tiny, mocking dance on the coarse grass. 'You can always tell my buildings – they're all over Hainaut and Brabant – because stylistically they subvert themselves a little, as things should.'

Robert thought: perhaps it is the solitude of this place, or the gulf of age and nation between us, which makes confidences easier.

Louis was saying: 'All that was three years ago – then I was an out-of-work divorcé. But the world is very considerate, Monsieur. It keeps on turning.' He touched Robert's arm, as if in consolation. 'Now I have a private consultancy and an angel-wife!'

As he turned back towards his tent, the Englishman smelt on him, oddly like incense, the faint fragrance worn by Josiane.

*THE NOTEPADS are the seed-bed from which the book will come. They contain details, pictures, thoughts. I write them sitting on these rocks in the starlight.*

*Today: the first day of freedom.*

*I cannot take on Inca perceptions. But can try to shed my own. And the first thing is to describe this land. If I concentrate, the commonplace will disperse. A matter of attention, and of openness. Let objects shape their own words. Then the book will come.*

*Afternoon: razor spurs, treeless. Grey-blue shale. Terrific, steely valley-sides. The complexity of this ravine: shifting light. Not a soul in sight, except two small girls by the Apurimac, who run away. From here the river flows almost 4,000 miles before it reaches the Atlantic. Even in August it's a torrent.*

*Camilla walks steadily. I'd feared she might tire. Always thinks I'm leaving her behind. We descend the ravine with a bamboo pole in either hand, like skiers over the dust.*

*Mystery: how the Spaniards conquered. Steel armour, Toledo swords, guts, war-horses, arquebuses: not enough against such disparity in numbers. Did the Inca think them gods?*

SHE WAS woken by the gravelly voice of the Belgian and thought he must be talking in his tent with Josiane. Then she saw the sleeping-bag crumpled beside her, and peered out.

Robert was settling among the rocks with his notebook under the stars. For several minutes she watched his bowed head and the flickering of his hand over the page. She knew he was starting his book, but these notepads were a mystery to her – he forbade her to read them. Before the intense, private passion of this writing, she felt herself recoil into practicality. She became the wife who worried over next year's school fees. She wondered too how she would feature in his narrative. But only as an airbrushed companion, she imagined, or a name lost in the acknowledgements.

She turned back to sleep, without bitterness. She did not think of herself as especially lovable. When her son was younger it might have been easier to imagine herself so. But now he was at boarding school – aged fifteen, his voice cracked – she instead felt intermittently bereft. She wanted him as a child, still.

When she curled up she was pleased to find no stiffness in her body. She flexed her back, pinched her calves: nothing. She did not want to let Robert down.

But often now, beneath the conventions of solicitude, she felt separate. Perhaps, to sense herself a woman, she needed somebody's dependency. For years after her son's weaning, she would wake up feeling a child at her breast.

THE TURMOIL in the Spaniard's mind was not anxiety but a feverish euphoria, heightened by the cruelty of this land, and by the strangeness of what he was doing. He was exhausted, but could not sleep. He looked as if he could bear nothing. Under the sheen of boyishly parted hair his eyes were black and flinching, and his features attenuated into a nervous fragility.

Gingerly he stood a candle on the groundsheet in the tent, and hung his crucifix above. Then he opened his breviary and read aloud the *Anima Christi*, to still his heart. Twice he lifted his eyes and asked forgiveness of the enamelled body hanging there on its cross, discoloured by the successive fingertips of his grandmother, his aunt, his mother. He grew calmer.

After a minute he felt in his rucksack and pulled out a disc of polished quartz. Cautiously he wiped its surface and saw again his reflection swimming in the candlelight. He had found it in the disc since boyhood: the troubled face. But now, inexplicably, it shocked him – his survival here; and he realised that he had half expected to find in the polished circle nothing at all.

Outside, the Belgian's laughter rolled out above the noise of the river. Francisco shuddered. These people carried their worldliness about with them like armour. Cities dripped from them. Nothing they said – no look, no gesture – escaped contamination. Louis in particular: those yellowing jowls and bulging, glandular eyes and easy talk about everything unnecessary! And just when you expected him to be serious, that dreadful laughter would detonate out of his chest as if to disinfect himself of truth.

Josiane, too. Could you be like that and yet alive? She would have been all right in porcelain. In fact he had seen her in shop windows in Trujillo – pale and sightless. Assistants changed her dress and wigs once a month. The thought of her touch frightened him.

Then there was the English couple. The journalist made you afraid to speak. If you did, he either dismissed or devoured you, demanding explanations. Those pale, hot eyes! Once that evening Francisco had ventured a word about the early Spanish missionaries, and Robert had machine-gunned him: Which ones? When? Where? What exactly . . .? His intensity was preferable to the Belgian's cynicism – he even looked sympathetic, with his long, responsive face and lips – but still it was unbearable. You longed to pass unnoticed. Yet a human being, Francisco was sure, was a God-made thing.

Only the Englishwoman, whose husband ignored her, seemed different. There was a stillness, a gravity about her. She had a comfortable, womanly body. She spoke graspable things. You could sense her by her eyes. Behind Josiane's – they were violet, long-lashed – you could not be sure who existed: they were only pretty. But against Camilla's brown skin her eyes shone grey and slanting. He decided she was beautiful.

After a while he unwrapped a book in a scuffed leather binding, *El Calvario del Inca: Crónicas contemporaneas*, and fondled it open. On its flyleaf was inscribed in faded ink the name of his mother, and beneath, in the same hand but wavering, weakened: '*Para Francisco, para que comprenda y se ilumine.*' He chose a page – like a talisman – at random.

*I moved across a good portion of this land and saw terrible destruction in it. I could not help feeling great sadness. The sight of such desolation would move you to great pity. We cannot conceal the paradox that the barbarian Inca kept such excellent order that the entire country was calm and all were nourished, whereas today we see only infinite deserted villages on all the roads of the kingdom.*

Francisco closed the book gently. He knew many such passages by heart.

# Two

ALL NEXT morning, circled by empty mountains, they wound for thousands of feet up the wall of the Apurimac valley, until their track tilted over a watershed to move above cloud-filled ravines. The going was hard from the start. It wrenched at unaccustomed muscles and chafed tender skin. But even after four hours' climbing they were laughing a little, and found the energy to sing beneath some *chilka* trees where they examined their feet for blisters. They looked back in wonder across the valley they had descended yesterday, tracing the hairline of their path where it wavered down a seeming precipice. A muted pride touched them. It looked possible only to goats.

Louis alone seemed disgruntled, as if his sturdy, rock-climbing horse were secretly tormenting him. Sometimes he clutched his back. While the English couple and the priest climbed sweating at the heels of the guide, he gave up steering his horse and let it turn the track's corners undriven. Camilla wondered what he and his wife had expected. Josiane rode in expensive-looking jeans and a lacy alpaca cardigan bought in Lima, while Louis wore a cream-coloured denim suit and fedora sunhat. Occasionally Josiane stopped to check her complexion in a little mirror. They had already taken a two-week cruise on the Amazon, and still they looked as if they were riding in some public cavalcade.

Often Louis ached to dismount, but knew that if he did he would lag far behind. So he watched Josiane, who floated in front of him with no visible effort at all, and found a purpose for this trek's foolishness in her delight at the landscape or at the antics of her horse. Sometimes she pointed a camera at some rearrangement of mountaintops, framed by trees or dusted in clouds. She had developed a faint, habitual smile. It was her holiday, after all: he would never have contemplated it. She expressed no surprise at the land's ruggedness, made no complaint. She simply watched it pass around her with the innocence that had touched him when they first met. Then he could only mock it or fall in love. Now he laughed at himself instead of her.

Sometimes he closed his eyes against the jarring hooves under him. The passion for landscape passed him by. The English kept exclaiming at this vista or that, while the Spaniard gazed ahead as if God were round the next corner. But to Louis the idea of scenic beauty was a bizarre confidence trick. These chilly peaks and shaley valleys! Nobody had admired such things before some fashion decided nature was sublime. And now troops of tourists wandered about exclaiming 'How beautiful!' It was an inherited delusion. Mountains were not beautiful, he thought. A Bach cantata might be beautiful, the Fontaine-bleau staircase was beautiful, Josiane was beautiful. But land was just geology.

He let his reins fall idle over the saddle's pommel. For miles ahead the track moved across a sheer cliff-face. Step two paces to the left, and you were gone. But they were all used to this now – they went in Indian file – and the horses walked with a surer tread than humans did.

He heard the Englishman, tramping in front of Josiane, trying to flirt with her. Their voices were thin above the ravine.

'You ride well.'

'We had horses in the Midi, my family.'

'I thought you were Belgian.'

'Louis is Belgian. I am French. From the Midi.'

French, Robert thought; that made her more graspable. Her horse's head kept nudging his back. Whenever he turned she flashed a blithe, full-lipped smile; yet it was as impersonal as semaphore. She baffled him. The unlikeli-ness of her being here – her child's fragility – suggested some hidden resource. She seemed at once vain and unworldly. Her hands holding the reins fascinated him. They were not a girl's hands at all, but lean and veined. He imagined electricity shivering into her horse's mouth. Their bones were as thin as harp strings.

It was odd to be talking like this, stranded in clouds. But he said: 'So your family lives in France.'

'My mother, yes. My sister has a business in Toulouse. She makes animals.' Her laughter trickled out across the abyss.

'Animals?'

But the guide was pointing now, his stick tracing some

feature near the horizon, and they tried to follow his gaze. Far ahead the clouds had congealed to lumps, and seemed to be pouring mountains out of the sky. Wave upon wave, the ridges hung there in jagged solitude, banked up like a tide, growing fainter, fading away. On one of them the guide was pointing out the Inca ruins of Choquequirau, but nobody else could see them.

For two more hours they curled round the mountain flanks, sometimes dropping into gullies lush with orchids and acacia. Then Robert saw in the distance what appeared to be the seamless rampart of a great fortress above the valley.

'There it is!' He turned to Josiane. 'You see it?'

She reined in her horse. 'Oh yes!' She smiled at it, as she had smiled at everything else – mountains, flowers, him. '*Quelle follie*! Why should they build it there? Up in clouds!'

But Robert didn't know. Nobody knew. The place had gone unrecorded, even by the Spaniards.

An hour later the jungle broke apart and they found themselves walking over grass beneath the curve of huge terraces. Dusk was falling. The distant rampart – an optical illusion – had separated into these stone esplanades hacked out from a forest whose trees they couldn't name. They camped exhausted on the lowest tier, where the muleteers had staked out their tents, and felt a childish sense of achievement: they had reached their first Inca city. Concealed under canvas, they massaged their legs and sucked vitamin pills, anointed reddened skin, bolted a few private rations.

Meanwhile the ruins lay above them, waiting for tomorrow, and the night came down in silence. Robert was jubilant. This was their first staging-post, and it was spectacular. Even from here he imagined it lying open like a book: an Inca city untouched by the intervening centuries, spread innocent on its mountain, its purpose unknown.

After supper, lying in their tent, his elation reached out to Camilla. He was not sure if the form doubled up in her sleeping-bag – she said it was cold now – was reconciled to this journey or accusing him for it. He said: 'You're not frightened, are you?'

She stirred slightly: 'No, not really. I'm just not used to this.' Then suddenly: 'Do you realise that it's jungle outside and we haven't heard a thing? It's utterly silent.'

But no, she thought, she wasn't afraid. Not of anything specific. Only she told herself: we are alone now. And now that she thought this, lying in the cold tent, she realised that what frightened her was emptiness. The idea of nothing. Didn't people have to be strong for a place like this? Or be able to protect one another? In other places the night was full of tiny, reassuring sounds. But here the stillness was the silence that underlay everything, always. In London she never noticed stars: the sky was orange. Now they chilled her. Could you disappear into this country and come out unscathed?

He said: 'Of course it's silent. It isn't rain forest.' But he heard the intolerance in his voice, and leant over and held her shoulders. 'There's nothing dangerous left here. It's almost uninhabited. The Shining Path guerrillas were mopped up years ago.'

She curled her arms slowly over her breast, her fingertips touching his. It's not that, she thought, it's nothing like that.

NONE OF them had seen anything like it. The Apurimac had reappeared from the east and was coiled six thousand feet vertically below them. Nineteenth-century travellers had imagined this place to be the lost Vilcabamba, but now, in the absence of record, the theories had all worn thin. Perhaps it had been the remote estate of a forgotten princeling, or a sanctuary where the last Inca ruler was raised by priestesses, the Virgins of the Sun; or perhaps a shrine for the mummies of the Inca royal dead.

They climbed the five terraces into a square edged by ruins. Their feet rustled over a plain of grass. Robert identified building-types from his reading, as if he were leafing through his memory. For the first time, the dead stirred into life. Here, preserved up to their eaves, were the long meeting-halls; above them a paved water-channel and the façades of immense storehouses; beside them the spouts and basins of a dry fountain. Under the beautifully jointed walls his enthusiasm became infectious. He overflowed with talking, and the others listened to him. 'Look, look!' They peered over to where the great terraces dropped into jungle. The Inca had shored up the soil against the mountains as if it were gold. 'The most successful agricultural empire on earth!' he heard himself saying. 'They gave us the potato, and pioneered dried vegetables. And you see up there?'

High above them, the granary chambers, with their multiple windows for ventilation, might have been the sleeping quarters of an army. All over the empire they had been built against famine. 'The Inca had a genius for organisation!' Their empire struck him as an administrative prodigy: a confederacy of peoples benignly enrolled under the supreme Inca. They paved ten thousand miles of roads between Ecuador and Chile. They built suspension bridges of aloe ropes moored on stone piers, and a relay of messengers could carry news over a thousand miles in a week.

His voice echoed in the gabled halls. The tenons which had secured their giant thatches were still in place. Here were all the architectural elements he had expected: the inward-leaning doorways with their monolithic lintels, the stone rings to hold doors now vanished, the trapezoidal windows and niches which broke up the monotony of the magnificent walls

Suddenly Josiane asked: *'Est-ce qu'ils n'avaient pas froid, là-haut?'*

'Cold?' Robert laughed. 'Well, yes, they probably were. But this stone . . . No civilisation in the world cut stone like the Inca! And they built without iron, without the wheel.' He was thinking of the great buildings he had examined in photographs. Many showed glossy, coursed masonry; others were composed of polygonal boulders, some weighing hundreds of tons, shaped and dovetailed without mortar and bevelled inward at the edges in a near-seamless jigsaw. Even here some of the doorways were of handsome ashlars. You couldn't slip a pin between the stones. The niches which gaped through doorways onto the square had perhaps held ancestral mummies. Louis ran his hands over them, muttering in surprise, while the *mestizo* guide walked away through the empty halls rolling a cigarette.

After a while Robert and Camilla were left alone there, with the priest hovering at their side. He had hung on Robert's words with a nervy concentration. Now he said in his soft, correct English: 'But the palaces must have looked . . . humble.'

'In what way?'

'Thatched. Like cottages.'

'The thatches were immense! And the walls look plain now, but some were stuccoed and painted, others were hung with tapestries of vicuña wool – and whole temples were sheathed in gold. Humble, no.' The priest's gaze was fixed on the ground. Robert went on: 'It was a rich civilisation, powerful. The conquest by your people – Spaniards, I mean – was astonishing.'

Francisco said very quietly: 'They were hard men. From Estremadura,' then added even quieter: 'That's where I come from.'

'From Estremadura?' Robert stared at him. 'Hah! Why didn't you say so before? That's extraordinary.'

The priest was blushing like a boy. 'I was born near Trujillo . . . the conquistador city. My father named me Francisco, after the conquistador leader Pizarro.' But now he wanted to escape their gaze: Robert's eyes blazing with inquiry, Camilla's soft, wondering.

She was thinking what an unlikely descendant of the conquistadors he was: a slip of a youth with his aquiline features and olive skin.

'Is that region still hard?' Robert demanded. 'Still poor?'

'It's all right for cattle and pigs.'

How could they understand? Francisco wondered. The land was not like this one, but a plateau spotted with gum-cistus and outcrops of grey rock, the cursing-stones of his father. Its pastures were matted in brown grass for half the year, and quartered by drystone walls which crumbled as quickly as you built them.

To him those fields were haunted by his father: a man on horseback, grasping a whip. In the boy's mind he rode round an infinite estate. His iron-grey hair was swept back from heavy brows. And always Francisco's memories converged on a single image: his father staring down from his saddle, his eyes shadowed under his cloth cap, but unswerving, angry. Because what he looked down on was disappointment: the watery maze of dreams and fears that was his younger son. '*How have you wasted your time today?*'

Camilla was asking: 'Your people were farmers, then?'

'Yes . . . yes.'

The cattle-shed had been bigger than their house at first: a grey-stoned barn for wintering and silage. The herd were pure white – you could stroke them – with small heads and blunt horns. But when he was ten they sold the place – his father called it 'a wilderness' – and bought the *Finca Santa Amalia de Abaja*. Wrought-iron gates hung on its pillars, and a smart fence ran barbed wire all around their land. Great buttresses supported the house walls, and he had his own room looking out on eucalyptus trees. That day he followed his father out to see the new cattle. They had curved horns and burnished red coats, and drank from a stone-lined waterhole. They were 'stronger stock', his father said.

Francisco said: 'I think I liked the white ones better.'

'The *white* ones!' His father's face had frozen into that terrible, livid glare. 'D'you think they're toys, then? By God, what's in your blood?' He had spurred his horse forward in contempt.

Camilla was asking: 'Were you an only child?' She seemed to pity him.

'I have an elder brother.' But now that Francisco had

been separate from his family so long, even Miguel shone in an odd half-light. It was Miguel, swaggering, to whom his father taught stockbreeding. And it was from Miguel, aged eight, that Francisco first heard the family boast of conquistador blood. 'Let's play Spaniards and Incas!' – and they wrestled in the stubbled fields, until he felt his twisted arm screaming against his shoulderblade. Miguel always won, yet never tired of this monotony. 'Who's Pizarro?' he would yell, and twist again until Francisco bleated, 'You are.' 'And who's the yellow Inca, Atahualpa?' His arm screaming again. 'I am . . . I am the yellow Inca, Atahualpa!'

Atahualpa. It was only a name then. But in school he learnt how the Inca emperor was captured by the conquistador leader Pizarro, and traded his freedom for a promise of gold heaped eight feet high up the wall of his cell. The Inca kept his word, but the Spaniard did not. Atahualpa was baptised, then executed.

'But what about Trujillo?' Robert was asking. 'Those old conquistador homes?'

'Trujillo is beautiful, if you like that sort of place.' Even to him his voice sounded fastidious, almost bitter. 'It is built of rock and granite. Everything rises from rock. There are conquistador houses and palaces there, yes. They came back rich.'

He had once loved the town, or felt in awe of it. He had thrilled to its fortified mansions and churches stacked up the hill against the abandoned castle, and he loved San Martín church where the storks still nested, its tower heavy with bells which sounded every quarter hour in a tinny crash like something hitting hollow armour. Especially he remembered how one evening his mother had led him up to where the Virgin Mary gazed over the town from her chapel window in the ruined castle. As they entered, his mother had pressed a hundred-peseta coin into his hand and guided it through a slot. 'She's your favourite,' she said. 'Our Lady of Victory.' She was smiling at him. He had inherited her fragile looks; but in her they were beautiful. Suddenly the chapel lit up and for a few minutes the Virgin Mary shone out over all Trujillo, even beyond. He thought: she is shining because of me! I have done this!

But next morning his father took him to the town square. He had a purpose, Francisco knew: his father always did. The boy became aware of the busts of conquistadors leaning from the walls in stone, their mouths open as if shouting or angry, flanked by twinned eagles and bears. They fascinated and repelled him. Then his father led him to the foot of the monstrous thing itself. On its plinth he read: 'Francisco Pizarro, conquistador', and gazed up.

Lifted thirty feet on his pedestal, and twice life-size, the conqueror rode in full armour. The boy observed him with a pang of fear, even of recognition. Far above, beyond the prehistoric head of the horse, the cruel eyes were shadowed by a raised visor. The sun streaming under it hacked the face into a jigsaw of jagged beard, hooked nose, grim mouth. A double plume streamed obscenely from his helmet.

Francisco's gaze dropped to the ground. Beside him his father put his arm around his shoulders, so that the boy shuddered at the unaccustomed warmth of it. His father was dedicating him, he knew. The boy began to shake. The hand on his shoulder was flecked with black hairs, its

29

nails blunted by work, yet almost tender. When Francisco stared up at the statue again, its eyes were vacant slits under lids coated in verdigris. Were they glaring? Or closed? He could not tell. Only the horse's eyes bulged insanely through its head-armour.

A light wind had sprung up and was rippling the grass in the empty square of Choquequirau. Robert was saying: 'But most conquistadors didn't return. They grew rich and settled here.' From a far wall the emptied niches shed down their memory of the Inca dead.

Tentatively Francisco asked: 'Do you think that what we did can be pardoned?'

Robert baulked. He did not think in those terms. He kicked irritably at the earth.

Instead Camilla asked gently: 'How did you become a priest?'

'I'm not really a priest,' he said. 'I'm just a seminarian, a deacon.' He looked back into her eyes, and imagined that he found something firm there, deep and firm. For a moment he trusted her. 'I've always wanted to be a priest.'

How to explain that from childhood God had cried out in the swell of the church organ beneath so many voices, cried out in the mysterious agony of the crucified, in the wafer that was His body? Even his father had knelt at the altar before the little balding celebrant – it was strange to see. Even his brother. So Francisco knew that there was nothing meaningful to be except God's servant. And in a side-chapel, above where Christ hung naked in his exquisite passion, Our Lady of Victory, Patroness of Trujillo, floated on silvered clouds. She had austere cheekbones and golden robes. And her grey eyes slanted down on him with a frightening promise.

'A deacon.' Camilla seemed to ponder this. 'How long is your training then?'

'Six years. I've already done five.'

It was in the seminary, a year ago, that he began to have nightmares – he could not tell the Englishwoman about those – until one morning, in the interval between Sacramental Theology and Penitence, he had suffered a breakdown. You could not explain it even to the Rector of the seminary, even to yourself, even to God. You could only go away for a time, and purge yourself – that was what they said – and promise to return. Sometimes God sent you on a journey.

He was afraid she might ask him something more. He would not lie to her. And her husband was pacing about like a chained animal, thinking things. Yet he wondered if already she might not understand. Almost in panic he reached behind him into his rucksack to find the quartzite disc. It came cool and precious to his fingers, and when he handed it to her it felt like a love-gift. It was his reward to watch her eyes dilate in wonder, and her hands fondle it. 'What is it?'

'It's an Inca mirror.'

She turned it over in her hands. 'Look, Robert, look.'

He came and stood between them. 'I've never seen such a thing.' His smile shed a glow of interest over Francisco, which made the deacon wince. 'Where did you find it?'

'It belongs with my father's family. He says our ancestors were conquistadors. He inherited a sword-hilt and a dagger as well, otherwise I would not think it true. My father kept no interest in the mirror. He let me take

31

it.' He passed his sleeve over its surface. 'I think it a beautiful thing.'

Robert took it from Camilla's hands, and they gazed by turn into its opaque surface. For a moment, as they lifted it to their faces, they wondered independently what they might see there. Both had a fancy that the darkly brilliant disc gave access to a different world, perhaps the past. Robert wondered: had the Inca too imagined that his reflected image loomed out of elsewhere? The face imitating his might be a mocking stranger.

But more likely in such mirrors, Robert thought, the Inca became self-conscious for the first time, and began to conceive himself as a separate being with an inner life. So mirrors bestowed identity. No wonder only nobles were permitted them. Fancifully he raised it on his palm, in the gesture of Inca offering. 'Who looked in this before, I wonder? The Virgins of the Sun? Atahualpa?'

Francisco received it back from him. The idea of Atahualpa's face there had never occurred to him. Had Pizarro's reflection then followed it? He felt faintly sick. He wiped its surface again, and folded it back in its cloth. Atahualpa. Some of the early chroniclers – from the books his mother lent him, or from the library in Plasensia – he remembered as clearly as his breviary or the Bible.

*'And Atahualpa was led out for execution to the sound of trumpets in the town square of Cajamarca, and he commended his sons to the governor don Francisco Pizarro. But the friars attending him advised him to forget his wives and children and to die like a Christian. But he continued to persist in commending his sons, with great weeping, indicating their size with his hand, showing by the signs he made and by his words that they were small, and that he was leaving them . . . and he said that yes, he*

*wanted to be a Christian; and he was baptised. With these last words, and with the Spaniards who surrounded him saying a credo for his soul, he was quickly strangled.'*

CAMILLA TRAMPED among the ruins alone. At first she thought that their bare walls and angular shapes were monotonous: no carving or domestic detail touched them with intimacy. In fact it was hard to believe that they had ever been other than ruins, or that a people had once cherished them. But gradually she noticed how they enshrined the world outside: how the landscape stood like paintings in their doorways, how a window framed a mountain – Robert said the Inca worshipped mountains – or consecrated the wanderings of the Apurimac. Compared with Robert, she knew nothing of the Inca, but she sensed this reverence, and imagined it a discovery of her own.

She climbed a path up a hill above the ruins. Once its summit had been crowned by a shrine or an observatory, but now she found grass and stray stones. She felt a strange release. The only sound was the wind in her ears. All around her swam a crowd of grey-blue mountains, and the river was slipping through black ravines a mile below. Here was only the savage and unmediated nature which had frightened her before. There was no birdsong. The river made a twist of silver through barren gorges, as if it were descending out of the first creation. Now that nobody could see her, she raised her arms and closed her eyes.

'THE QUIPU,' Robert read, '*was a circlet dangling knotted strings of various lengths and colours. By this means, in a system now lost, the Inca sent their messages. Spaniards recorded them reading off their quipus like a book. But in fact the device confined itself to simple data and numbers. It recorded no feeling and no complex thought: only the arithmetic of facts.'*

'And that's what language should be!' Louis proclaimed. 'Anything more points a civilisation to misery. Hah–hah! Forgive me.' He squeezed Robert's arm. 'I forgot your profession. But tell me, have you written yet, have you written?'

Robert laughed. But he was still not used to Louis. Beneath the man's playfulness simmered something which made him wary. Now Louis sat exhausted in the shadow of a wall, his fedora tilted to one side, sipped from his hip-flask and said: 'Myself, I have no energy even to breathe here, let alone write.' He inhaled noisily. 'What altitude are we at, do you suppose?' He flung out an arm at the valley below them. 'Look at that! Wouldn't that move an ape to words? You should write here, Monsieur, if you can't write here . . .'

But Robert sensed that Louis despised landscape. He said: 'I'm just making notes.' And suddenly he wanted to be alone and – yes – to possess this place in words. The ruins were full of secluded spots. And there was time.

But Louis went on: 'If you ask me, the genius of the Inca lay not in what they created but in what they *refused* to create. The wheel! Think what trouble the wheel has caused! And writing. They had no writing, did they? What a tragedy the alphabet has been!'

Robert took the flask he offered, and found himself drinking a rich Cognac. It trickled lava through his veins. Perhaps it was the altitude, he thought, but either the drink or the healing air made it easier for him to suppress his irritation and to adopt Louis's flippant tone. 'Yes, who would invent writing? As a journalist, I know. It's nothing but slippage.' He drank again – a ghostly toast to the mountains – and handed the flask back. 'Here's to *quipus!*'

Louis murmured '*Salut!*', lifted the flask, then pulled his hat over his eyes, and fell asleep.

ROBERT MOUNTED a stairway which ended, mysteriously, in nothing. He was conscious of the pain in his blistered feet. A copse gave a view of the river valley and of the city's skeleton below him – everything he wished to see. To evoke this, he knew, carried a peculiar importance. To the Inca, the country before him was not stone and jungle but a living map whose contours traced an intricate web of sanctities. From the Inca epicentre at Cuzco, the Temple of the Sun, a fan of invisible power-lines had radiated out along chains of hallowed mountain summits, rivers, and massive, isolated rocks, to the farthest limits of the empire. So the whole land might have been read like a holy text.

He cleared a space and sat with his back against an *alyssos* tree. Once he looked up and saw a hummingbird quivering beside the branches above him. He took it as an omen. The wind had dropped, and in this perfect, suspenseful silence he opened his notebook and started to write.

He wrote in short, jagged sentences as the images came to him, seized by an unexpected urgency as if time were running faster at this height. He had no planned narrative. But he knew that he must record this site now, before tomorrow's trek sapped his will and it slipped away. He was conscious, too, of writing with an angry defiance, against age, against Louis, against his own fears. And he wrote for a long while – not impressionistic notes, but finished paragraphs (he imagined) wrested out of the elusive valleys beneath, the Inca stones, and the silent river. The scene struck him as so grand and so complex that it demanded both a wide descriptive sweep and a rather sophisticated exactitude. He knew, too, this moment's importance: that it was a litmus test for his future. In fact if he stopped to think, he might panic that the rest of his working life was being presaged here, in this unknown ruin under the *alyssos* tree. He had not written so freely, almost violently, since adolescence. He felt all his learnt constrictions dropping away. For the first time in years he was writing for no readership but himself.

For a long time he continued in a kind of frightened euphoria. The dipping sun began to dazzle him through the branches. At last he eased back exhausted, uncertain of what he had done. The silence was complete. He closed his eyes. He felt his notebook throbbing under his hand, but he did not read it.

After a while voices sounded on the terraced stairway behind him. They belonged to Louis and Josiane. He wondered how they talked when they were alone, wondered how she looked at him. Then he heard her voice – light, teasing – say: '*Tu es simplement envieux, Lou-Lou. Toi, qui ait du talent mais qui manques de volonté*' – and Louis's laughter went on rumbling until her words became inaudible.

Robert waited for the silence again, then picked up his notebook to read what he had written.

At first he could not believe it. He thought his early sentences must be preliminary mistakes. So he read on more quickly, waiting for the sentences to take fire, the sentences he remembered. But he found only lifeless words. They never left the page. They coated it with a language so lustreless that it was near to cliché. Only a few bubbles of pretension marked where something original had tried to surface.

He felt a bitter bewilderment. He wondered if he were exhausted, numb. It was like reading undeciphered script.

He read again, slowly, tried a few corrections, gave up. Worse, this writing brought an ache of recognition, almost of despair. It was strenuous, serviceable, his own. But it could not make the world new. It could not evoke this land of torrent and precipice. Everything he'd ever written, ever said or thought – everything written by everybody else – overhung it in a stale cloud. He thought: I'm locked into these phrases, these rhythms. I can't escape them.

But he knew he would try again. And again. Already he had settled back to outstare this landscape. There must, after all, be descriptive solutions to all these things: how ridges cut into river valleys, how clouds alter mountains. There must even be perfect definitions. He tried very coolly to write them now. He tried to analyse the cloud patterns on the slopes opposite, how they redefined the ridges as they moved.

But they remained ungraspable. He watched them slip between his words. He thought: the lexicon is too thin. The words for this landscape do not exist. He could not watch these mountains without a spasm of awe, but when he looked at what he had written he turned hot with frustration. It was as if a fog arose between the thing and its expression, blurring its precision, dimming its life.

He glimpsed the figure of Camilla on the spur opposite.

She looked tiny above the ravine. He could not tell what she was doing. In the ruins, the light was beginning to fade. He put away his notebook and the tension left his body. He saw the first stars appear. This, he thought, was the stillness he had forgotten. He had promised himself to pay attention. Let things themselves speak. Only listen. Idly, a little fancifully, he looked down at the darkening Apurimac, on its complicated weave between cliffs, and waited for natural sentences to form. He thought: it must be painless really, simple. It has nothing to do with originality. It is more like translation. Listen.

But he listened in paralysis. He was very tired now, and nothing came to him at all. Even when he thought about the Inca ruins, only the obvious occurred to him: the reiteration of architectural motif, the deifying of nature. Perhaps he had worked too long only with facts, because this unknown place suggested nothing beyond them. His imagination had gone dead. As he scratched out the descriptions in his notepad, he noticed his own hands, spotted with mosquito bites: how lumpily their veins stood up, how his finger-joints straightened into leathery pouches. They looked too old to begin again.

He salvaged nothing from what he had done. Only, in anger, he scrawled beneath: '*So I'm no damn good.*'

THAT NIGHT he heard Camilla singing in her sleep. It was a stifled, squeaky sound, but he could make out its rhythm, and a few words. The song was one which had become a signature tune between them, establishing itself by senti-mental fluke. It marked their chance reunion on a London Underground train. In the tent's dark he could discern the worried knot between her eyes while her lips were moving.

He had noticed the woman at once. She was very young. She wore a sleeveless summer dress. In the crowded train, with one arm raised to grasp the bar above, her shoulder lifted into view the start of one discreet breast. At first the nagging idea that she was familiar to him smacked merely of wish-fulfilment.

The tilt of her grey eyes against the brown skin – an illusion of their lids, he later decided – should have reminded him. Her eyes made a soft blaze. They were what you remembered after the rest of her had blurred. But they hadn't yet looked at him. Later, he thought, it was these eyes – intense and a little grave – which intimately bound him to her. In the din and rush of his journalist friends, she was the still centre, whose habitual, teasing, 'Do you think that's really true?' was to root him for years in some sort of integrity.

The girl was preoccupied, oblivious. Only on a crowded Underground, he thought, could you stand a foot from the armpit of a beautiful stranger. But the idea that she was not quite a stranger persisted. In the end it was one of her hands – it had a distinctive mole between thumb and forefinger – that triggered his memory. He had last seen her six years ago, when her face and body still hovered in girlhood. Then her parents had moved away from his neighbourhood in Kent, and he had forgotten her.

Even now, because he was not sure, he stood a little behind her and softly sang the absurd song from their childhood:

*Somebody stoked up the sun*
*Somebody lit up the moon . . .*

She turned round in surprise, suspicious, her adult eyes on him.

He said: Camilla?'

'Stephen?'

'Robert.'

'Oh,God, I'm sorry. Robert.'

'Who's Stephen?'

'Oh, nobody.' Laughter. Laughter he remembered.

Then came the formal kissing, the instant news round-ups – he overran his station by four stops – and shouted telephone numbers. As her smeared-glass profile eased away towards Marble Arch, he imagined her casting him a lifeline. He despised himself for this. But his mother had been dead only four months, and his father was in premature decline. Fragile, volatile, he had hurled himself into work. His quests, passions, iconoclasms threatened to run amok. Twenty years later he was still obsessed by time passing, by how the world's diversity could never fit into the span of a life. If his father had died at fifty-five, then how long . . .?

But in Camilla, he felt, he had recovered his stability, even his past. He had loved her – years ago – with the rapt, total love of somebody fulfilled in their deepest psyche. In her he had stopped time.

But when she woke up she could not remember what in her dream had made her sing.

# Three

NEXT DAY they thrust their way through cloud forest round the sheer mountain flank, leaving the river far behind. The sodden trees rasped and tore at the mules' packs as they struggled up, while an overgrowth of lichens and creepers swept the faces of the riders until they were forced to dismount, Josiane in silence, Louis groaning and floundering.

Towards noon they emerged opposite the high eastern ranges, along a track where even the mules trod delicately. Clouds seethed up from the ravines under their feet. Louis and Josiane trudged behind their horses, bedraggled and quiet, while the guide raked the mountains with his stick, shouting their Inca names. Across the horizon the summits of Vilcabamba covered the sky in an unearthly rampart. They looked impossible to penetrate. Clouds stormed like cannon smoke along the nearer ridges, and sent up giant smoke-signals into the artificial blue of the sky. Occasionally rain pattered down. Only the farthest peaks stilled the clouds to cumulus above streaks of snow.

By evening they had descended to a gully of the Rio

Blanco; but two years before an avalanche had flooded it with rocks, and the muleteers felt afraid – the valley was excitable, they said. So they pitched camp high above, and all next day laboured up through thick forest to the pass of Minas Victorias. The way was steeper and longer than anyone had anticipated. There was no yard of level ground. The euphoria of starting out had sobered into a dogged, sombre mood. Sometimes they looked at the heights ahead of them in disbelief. Their exclamations grew fewer and jokes sputtered out. Their breathing hammered them into silence. Josiane and Louis were on horseback again, but Louis's spine ached and his thighs ceased to grip.

Often the abrupt changes in altitude caught them all unawares. Towards noon they would be sweating in open sunlight, but at evening they went shivering after anoraks or pullovers buried in mule-packs carried far ahead of them.

They were starting to conserve themselves. Turn an ankle or inflame a knee, and you would have to sit a horse for a week while one of the muleteers led you out. Any throb or twinge left a spasm of foreboding.

Instead of their becoming conditioned, Robert wondered if they were not growing weaker. His own body had slackened and dulled, he knew. It was being infected by the numbness of his mind. Often he refused to look at the mountains any more: their formations only tormented him. They had shrunk to clichés. Instead he clamped his gaze on the guide's boots trudging ahead. His senses seemed wrapped in insulating tape. He could not form a sentence or even an image. The cartilage of one knee – an old trouble – had started to throb, and after the first day's descent his toes had swollen under blackened nails. He did not much care. His frustration made a dull, obliterating confusion in his chest.

The women were outlasting the men. Josiane, on horseback again, seemed to float oblivious above the track; occasionally she stopped to take a snapshot, and once or twice she opened her compact and smiled at the face there. Camilla watched her in astonishment. She thought she envied her a little: envied the sheer, light-worn youth of her, her girl's complexion, her blithe riding skill. But that innocent voice irritated her, as if it were pitched an octave too high. The violet of her eyes, she supposed, was the tint of contact lenses. She wanted to decide about Josiane, but couldn't. And Robert had noticed her.

As for herself, she was glad she went on foot. She felt a cautious confidence in her body, which was enduring everything without much hurt. Each morning she flexed her legs expecting stiffness, but found none. It was no trouble keeping pace with Francisco, or even with Robert, who was clouded in some dilemma of his own. He would not share it, she knew. So a little to her surprise she detached herself and imagined instead that she was accompanying her son into these mountains. He came with her not as a youth, but as a child: somebody she led by the hand.

And she thought: I don't have to love what Robert loves. I prefer the intricacy of these shrubs – tubular bells, purple and red – to the bleak summits. And mauve-tinted orchids everywhere. Cactus like spiky ping-pong bats. Hideous, really. Lupins and snapdragons, as if we strolled through a cottage garden. Flocks of parakeets flittering and screaming out of the treetops. I hadn't expected this. I can't remember what I had expected. Whatever Robert described, I suppose: something austere. Not these details of beauty in the cloud forest. And not this mountain air (it must be that) which expands and disengages you while you walk above the chasm. In the end it may not be good for you, of course. It empties you of too much old self, too much that has been settled and depended on. It cannot last. Just an experiment. Soon it might turn you heartless, retract your love into yourself. (So you grow stronger.) And it seems as if it has been waiting to happen for a long time.

As THEY pitched camp close under the pass of Minas Victorias, they noticed a schist-like dust glittering under their feet. The ground looked raw and misshapen. The slopes around them gaped with the shafts of abandoned mines. Here, said the guide, the Spaniards had used the Inca as forced labour. He broke open a stone from some nearby debris. It gleamed in the fading light: silver. One of the muleteers grimaced and muttered something as he carried brushwood past, something the guide translated without a smile: 'He says: this is an evil place. The Spaniards pissed on us here.'

Outside the dining-tent the cook had lit a fire to repel mosquitoes. In its smoky scent the trekkers sat exhausted, while he brewed up quinao soup with a hash of dry chicken and mountain potato. The huddle of their aluminium chairs, the candlelit table spread with its native cloth, and the protective presence of the guide (they paid him attention now) turned supper into an exhausted benediction, touched with the evening's peace. When Francisco murmured a private grace, they all remained standing. Small luxuries circulated. Louis shared his Cognac, and occasionally his laughter rolled out again; Camilla, with an ironic joke, passed round Belgian chocolates; Francisco offered a scented lotion for disinfecting their hands. And when the cook produced guavas and bananas in a light vanilla yoghurt, they cheered as if after all they carried civilisation with them.

Later, unable to bear Robert's silence, Camilla wandered out over the scree. The night was windless, cool. Their tents made illumined domes and triangles over the uneven ground. A rash of stars shone before moonrise. She looked at them now without love or recoil. She fancied they had grown used to her. In this light, if she kicked the path under her feet, it sent up a silvery powder. She stood for a minute with her back to the slope, looking down into darkness. The air was cold on her face.

Then, in the silence, she thought she heard a sound. It was resonant but indistinct, like the beat of a distant gong. It seemed to come from inside the mountain. At first she dismissed the thought, but then she heard it again. Yes: the mountain was echoing from inside. She turned round. Behind her the adit of a mine made a dark gash in the cliff. She wondered if it held bats. Near Cuzco she had seen horses whose napes had been opened raw by bats. But when she listened again, she heard nothing. Tentatively she approached the entrance. It made a thin arch in the rock face, barely taller than herself. It was overhung by *ichu* grass, like pale hair, and limned with ferns.

Then she heard the sound again. It was farther away now, or deeper buried: the disembodied voice of a man. She froze. Under the rock arch the last starlight faded. She wondered whether to call Robert. But then she thought:

the muleteers must be in here, talking. Perhaps they're trying to prise out silver. Or maybe vagrants live there.

But she knew there were no vagrants. This region was deserted. The mines had been abandoned years ago, and the tunnel looked unused. She stared into its blackness. Somewhere water dripped with a tiny, metallic echo. The cold made her shiver. Then, with a twinge of alarm, she noticed a glow of light. Its source was invisible, but an orange mist had crept over the walls. The voice started up again, melancholy, alone. And she recognised it. It belonged to Francisco.

She had the strange idea that he was hearing confession. The guide must be Christian after all, and even the muleteers. Who else would he be talking to? Josiane? Or had he gone mad?

She had no business to be here, she knew; but what if he were unwell? Now that her eyes were accustomed, she began walking down the corridor of amber light: a passage through the living rock, glistening with damp. Her outspread hands fumbled over walls of jagged stone. The ceiling, left low for Inca workers, scraped her head. Nothing remained but a few pit-props, and the slots for vanished beams. She stopped outside the circle of light. The words came distinct now, and from their Spanish flow she understood enough.

'. . . Lord, forgive us . . . that the souls of the dead find rest here . . . Forgive us . . .'

He was kneeling where three tunnels converged. A candle glimmered on the ground nearby. It sprawled his shadow monstrously over the rock wall. He had not heard her come. His black anorak and baggy trousers made her think he knelt there in a cassock. Suddenly ashamed, she backed away. Her feet scraped on the rock, but he did not hear. His own words were shaking him. His hands were locked together, quivering against his stomach, his whole body shaking, his shadow shaking on the wall.

To her horror she cried out: 'Francisco!'

He went still. But he did not stand up or turn round, only asked calmly: 'Who is it?'

'Camilla.'

His head was still bowed. 'Camilla.' He seemed to be tasting the sound.

'Are you all right?'

Then he turned to stare at her. His eyes looked too huge in the fragile face. They might have been weeping. They went on gazing at her. She had the idea that he was asking her forgiveness too.

'All right? Yes . . .'

To her own surprise she said: 'You can't take on everyone's sins, Francisco.'

He stared back in confusion. He seemed at once to accept and deny her. Quietly he said: 'These were not your people. I am a Spaniard. We committed these things. You are American. You did not.'

She said softly: 'I'm English.' It sounded, for some reason, like an overture.

'You are English, of course. But you didn't do this.'

'We did other things.'

He seemed not to hear. He was still kneeling, staring up at her. She wanted him to get to his feet, but he didn't. He said: 'Can you imagine what was committed in these places? How do you know how many died, how many Christians? The Inca were converts, you know. But who may say what they were? They were human souls.' His

47

eyes seemed to be sweating. 'Have you heard of the Potosi mine? That was the worst place. A city of slaves, bigger than your London, where silver was exchanged for human life. We did that everywhere.' He intoned, as if from a book: "*To complete the perdition of this land, there was discovered a mouth of hell, into which a great mass of people enter every year and are sacrificed.*" The words rang down the galleries. 'The men of my land did this. They made glory from it. All my childhood I heard about it. How glorious the sons of Trujillo were. How the conquistadors created an empire and made Spain rich with silver! But whose silver, we never asked.'

She said: 'That was long ago. Nearly five hundred years ago.'

'It went on for centuries. Silver and mercury . . .' He stood up, unclasped his hands. He seemed at last to become a man. Yet he looked so thin, so shaken, she wanted to touch him.

He said: 'Did you see those collections of silver in Lima, what was created out of these mines?'

'Yes, I did.'

'What did you think?'

'I found them ugly.'

'Yes, ugly!' He was exultant. She had realised. Like him she had understood how heinous they were: silver spun into fantastical table ornaments and dinner services, or beaten into solid candelabra. And those other, terrible things: the processional crosses and reliquaries, the monstrances and censers. Silver crowns for Our Lady. Silver-coated altars and retables. And priests – his own kind – had drunk the blood of the Saviour out of those silver chalices.

Absolution out of sin, life out of death. Christ must have abandoned them.

He bent down to pick up the candle, then put it back where it was. Instead he crossed himself and dedicated it to the dead: to the miners who had slaved in stench and din by the light of tallow candles, only to fall to their end from rotted hide ladders; to those who had died coughing up blood and mercury, or racked by pneumonia on the freezing surface.

Then he thought how beautiful she looked in the candlelight, how austere but compassionate her eyes were: a slanted mystery. He realised she was talking about mines – 'In those days they were like that in half Europe' (she was guessing, she wished Robert were here) – but he did not feel her absolving him. He did not want that. He wanted her understanding and her condemnation.

He said: 'If I were an ordained priest I would say Mass for their souls. What we did here – even God may not yet have forgiven us.'

She frowned unsurely. He looked very young to have access to God. His skin was smooth as ivory. Tentatively she said: 'Is that why you came on this journey, Francisco? Is it some kind of penance?'

'I became unwell. I should have been ordained by now. But I became sick.' He took a step towards her. She stepped involuntarily back, felt the hard rock at her shoulders.

She only said: 'I see.'

He gazed at her like a supplicant. Why could he tell her these things? He didn't know. 'My confessor said I needed healing. A kind of purgation.'

She asked gently: 'Are you well now?' She had not

meant to recoil from him. He was no threat. And he was, in his strange way, handsome.

'The Rector told me I could return to the seminary when I was well. But it is not easy to know. Not at all.'

He looked so vulnerable, no older than her son. His hair fell lankly over his ears. 'Perhaps you should find help.'

'I have help.' He touched his pocket, and she imagined a cross there.

'Of course.' But she realised she did not understand. There was something else here, she knew, something other than Christian or colonial conscience; but whatever it was eluded her. He was walking a labyrinth she could not follow. She only asked: 'How did you learn so much about the Inca?'

'A poor country boy, you mean!' A spark of anger had shot up. But as soon as he had spoken it, it died. 'My mother's family were not farmers. She was a secondary-school teacher. She still has a whole library.' He spread his arms. 'Now she is unwell, like me, but only in her body. She has *enfisema*. It was her money which paid for my journey. It's strange . . .'

'What's strange?'

'She is not a Christian. She doesn't believe at all. It was years before I knew that. She sees everything as history.' He turned round, as if someone might be listening. But there was no sound except the distant dripping of water.

Camilla wondered vaguely what Robert was doing, and whether to go back. Every time Francisco's candle guttered, their shadows lurched over the walls. And he was gazing at her again with that unsettling wonder.

He asked: 'And you? Why are you here? You have nothing to do with this country.'

'I'm here because of my husband. He's writing a book.'

'What kind of book?'

'He wants to do something new.'

'Why?'

The question startled her. 'He's like that.'

Francisco put Robert from his mind. He could not think of her in anybody's arms. She was still standing like a statue with her back to the rock. Her grey eyes made a soft fire. The candle lit high, sculptural checkbones. Perhaps God had sent her. He wondered if his love for her — he already called it that — might be the pure love he had imagined even in the seminary: love disinfected of all pride, all eroticism, all self. If only he could distil this feeling into innocence, leach out its darkness, he would be left with something transparent, holy. In this fine woman. Just for now, just for the length of a journey. He said: 'So you did not want to travel here.'

'My husband likes me here.'

Francisco thought angrily: but he ignores her. He's obsessed only by his own ideas. He said: 'I see.' But he did not see. He was celibate after all — as a priest he would always be — and he wondered if he could ever understand. Perhaps all marriages were mysteries. Marriage was a sacrament, after all.

Camilla too thought how odd — and past — her own words sounded. As if she had once been Robert's secretary or dog. And when she saw Francisco's face ignite with indignation, she felt obscurely grateful. There was something exquisite about him, even about the hands he now lifted abstractedly to his face. But she said: 'I should get

back. My husband will be wondering where I've gone.'
For some reason she would not tell Robert.

'Yes, yes.' But Francisco felt panic. Once they were out
of here, out of this sanctuary, she would revert to who she
had been before, integrated among the daylit others. He
wanted terribly to touch her. His hands left his face, but
then trembled to his sides.

She noticed this, and even imagined them on her
cheek. She felt an indefinable sadness.

She said: 'We'd better go back.'

# Four

THREE HOURS' suffering was enough to reduce them all to a myopic focus on routine. For five more days they climbed and descended like robots, their minds numbed, their eyes fixed on the track. If anyone stopped to exclaim at the view, it was secretly because his legs were throbbing unbearably, or lungs gasping. They concentrated only on their footfalls between the stones or over the black earth under the cloud forest. The ache in their muscles changed with the changing gradient. The downward slopes jarred their knees; ascending blistered their heels. And now a faint alarm was spreading among them, as if by contagion. They realised there was no going back.

Only the muleteers were immune. Patiently loading their animals, they started out long after the others, overtook them towards noon, and pitched camp hours before the exhausted trekkers reached them. Late at night the Europeans would hear them chatting in their glottal Quechua tongue, and catch their lilting laughter. They seemed to grow more tender to the group as it tired. The routine never varied. At six o'clock in the morning they brought bitter *cholita* coffee to each tent, waking its occupants with soft cries; after half an hour, an enamel bowl of warm water arrived; by seven o'clock a breakfast of coconut-flavoured cereals, and soon afterwards the group would be on its way.

Every sunrise the Europeans would gaze with awe at the mountains which had been blurred by their fatigue the previous day. Then the profiles that had surrounded them unseen at nightfall would detach themselves like mist patterns in the dawn, or transform to a silver line strung along the sky, where the sun struck weakly across their summits. They would hear the distant rush of some remote tributary of the Amazon, or a waterfall hanging in the cliffs. But within an hour or two, so steep was the track, they would be registering nothing but violent changes of terrain. They were being rocked on a giant switchback. From a mountain flank matted only by grass, they would climb within minutes to a valley which the moistening cloud had puffed into jungle, sopping with mist and ancient trees.

To Robert the mountains seemed to be turning malign. Avalanches had rushed down them, snapping or uprooting everything in their way. He noticed he was growing careless. Once he left his compass behind on a rock – the muleteers retrieved it – and twice he fell headlong over tree roots, which left him shuddering. For miles the track wound along precipices whose edges were obscured by a fickle fringe of brush. Any slip, and you could crash through this for hundreds of feet before a tangle of bamboo stopped you, cut to ribbons. Along the rivers, black mosquitoes left lumps of inflamed flesh beneath every bite.

Once only they passed a village of Quechua potato farmers, whose cottages were thatched as their Inca ancestors had thatched them. Tiny women in layered pink and crimson skirts came out shyly to stare, and a few men shook hands with a soft, formal clasp. Their presence in this wilderness should have been reassuring, yet was not. Pinched, silent, they seemed like ghosts in it.

Whenever he was forced to dismount, Louis settled to a pace of dull enduring. The more remote this country became, the more it repulsed him. And he was holding back the others, he knew – even Josiane, who clambered ahead of him with little mewing gasps. His hips and thighs – all the pampered years – weighted and constricted him. It was all very well for these others, but he was fifty-nine. And now he listened to his heart. It stormed alarmingly against his ribcage. It was encased in too much flesh. At any moment he imagined it imploding into a *boeuf bourguignon* of valves and pistons. He even felt sorry for it, as if it were independent of him. At every second turn of the track he would stop, while its pounding – noisier than anything in this detestable land – quietened down.

Only Robert was intermittently attempting something in his mind. His knee cartilage was throbbing ominously, but from time to time he still stared back at the mountains and ravines and hunted for words. He was glad that nobody voiced wonder at them any more. He could face their intransigence alone. In the morning, before setting out, he would again start to write, tensely. But the end was always the same. It must be a failure of imagination, he thought. You come into a valley where a tributary of the Amazon is flowing. Behind you the whole Apurimac watershed is on the horizon. But when you try to write, the land seems to hold some essence you cannot touch. Perhaps it was the play of cloud and light which defeated him, he thought. Or the sheer size of things: maybe the English vocabulary was not made for them. Their presence all around him was destructive of anything but stupefaction. Clichés stuck on him like grime. It would be better to write after he got home, perhaps, when the shifting lights were still.

But maybe it was not even important. The mountains were not a map of Inca thought, after all, not an explanation. At evening he sat out on the rocks again. He wondered if he could blame the starlight for this writing. His words wobbled over the page like someone else's.

TONIGHT: *I ask the guide to assemble the muleteers, and talk. They gather reluctantly: not hostile, but squatting in the tent, bewildered. Broad, tranquil faces. If you struck them, would they smile?*

*What do I want? I don't know: some clue from them, some chance idea, memory. Can't shake off the notion that they are withholding a secret. This is idiotic: the illusion of passive expressions.*

*Two of them scarcely speak. The other three chatter. Slithery, hypnotic language. Often sounds like chanting. In every word the penultimate syllable rings out like a little gong. Maybe it's these rhythms that tease you into thinking the Inca speech might have been recorded in the ideograms of cloth or pottery.*

*I ask about this, but nobody responds. Just blank.*

*I ask if this country is still holy to them. And do the patterns of Inca ruins remind them of anything? They frown. Blank. This is not their land, they say. Not their homeland.*

*I think of their breathy flute-playing, and ask: are there no words to their music? Had there never been? One of them — a taller man named Yupanqui — just says there are good pop songs in Lima. He turns on his transistor radio, and we hear only static. The others laugh.*

*The guide interprets all this with a curled smile, weary. Can't tell if he is patronising them or me.*

*Yupanqui: an aristocratic Inca name. Yet this muleteer merely says: 'I'm a big man in my village.'*

*They disperse with relief. The guide only tells me: 'You're wasting your time.' The cook remains mute throughout.*

*Some scholars believe there was an Inca language known only to the nobles: a language extinguished in the Spanish conquest. But how could it have vanished so utterly?*

*Linguists find no trace of it in modern Quechua. So perhaps it existed only in unvoiced signs, inscribed on perishable wood or cloth. A kind of silent music. Or pure memory.*

# Five

HAD IT been wrong to crave experience? His affairs had been fleeting and discreet. He felt he had chosen wisely, and Camilla had not known. Even on their first evening in Peru he had wandered Lima alone, and had gone into a nightclub near the Plaza de Armas.

He was seated in an aisle of candlelit tables, mostly empty. The walls were muralled with a self-conscious decadence: disembodied eyes, demons, kitsch nudes. A few businessmen murmured together; beyond them, a group of younger people in jeans and bomber jackets. The place seemed undecided whether it was a disco or a hostess nightclub.

She sat in a simple black dress. She had lustrous hair and dark skin, a little blemished. He could see her legs under the table. He ordered a Pisco Sour. A trio of musicians started to play plangent Inca music on panpipes and a flute.

Perhaps it was the drink which went to his head, because when he next looked at his watch it was almost eleven. Camilla would be lying in bed at the hotel,

worried. The woman was wedged between two custom-
ers, who were arguing across her. As he got up to leave
she asked: '*Me invita a un trago, señor?*' She uncrossed her
legs. They were long and lithe.

'I'm sorry. I have no time.'

'*Otra noche, quizás?*'

'I hope so, yes. Another evening.'

Long after he had left the club he was irked by this
remembered longing, by incompleteness. As if a space had
opened up in him, and nothing had entered it.

He remembered this as he watched Josiane descending
to the stream at evening. He was surprised that she had
such stamina at the end of the day, she looked so slight.
Soon afterwards he saw the flash of her camera in the dusk.
He had the guilty notion that she was photographing him
as he followed. But instead he found her kneeling near the
water, snapping the madonna lilies which trickled along its
banks.

'*Imaginez si on avait des fleurs pareilles chez nous! On ne les
voit que dans des boutiques de luxe!*'

He crouched beside her. He had nothing to say about
the lilies. They looked uninteresting, too closed up, and all
alike.

'But they are not alike,' she said.

'How do they differ?'

But she only laughed – a dry tinkle – as if he were
blind.

He scrutinised her flagrantly. Why was she so private?
Her slimness was hidden under a chunky pullover and
thick trousers. Her sunhat lay on the ground. It had
crushed her hair close round her face into a semi-circle of

blonde cowlicks. Her ingenuous smile broke confusingly from full, rather sensuous lips.

'You photograph everything,' he said.

'If I don't, I will forget. I will forget that I was here.'

'Not really '

'Not really.' The tinkle of laughter again.

So photographs were memory, not compositions. All the same, she kept readjusting the angle and focus of her camera, shifting to a new plant.

He said: 'You should be tired out.'

'It is a very hard journey. Harder than our time on the Amazon. It worries me.'

For some reason he felt a touch of alarm. 'Why?'

'Because of Louis. He is not young, you know.'

He agreed, cruelly. 'I know.'

She said childishly: 'I think he may get cross with me.'

'Cross with you?' You might as well be angry with a flower.

'You see, it was my idea. I like very much to ride. But these horses are wrong. They are very strong, but they feel nothing. You can't guide them.' Her English, he noticed, was growing more fluent, leaving little French but the lilt of a nasal accent. Shyness, he supposed, had prevented this before.

He felt an urge to provoke her, to press her into revelation. 'How did you two meet?'

'We met on holiday.' Her laughter placed a full stop here. She pocketed her camera. 'And you. Camilla is strong, I think, happy. She seems not to mind this.'

'Happy?' He wondered if that was right: was Camilla happy?

'Yes. More than us all. More than Francisco.'

61

'Well, Francisco's strange.'

'Maybe he is only very young.' Nothing she said was quite expected; at first he had attributed this to the awkwardness of language, but now he was not sure. He wondered again about her age. She could be scarcely older than Francisco, could she? He glanced down at her hands. They were white, flawless, their fingers ending in opalescent nails as if she had just stepped from a manicurist's. Their only blemish was the marriage ring.

She got to her feet with a small moan. He wanted to delay her. He was used to feeling women respond. Arrogant, yes, if you like (that was Camilla's charge). He had imagined Josiane like a sun-fish swimming into his net; but in fact she was an eel, immaculate and cunning (for all he knew), gliding through it and away. His voice sounded rough to him: 'So what do you do back in Belgium? Do you have children?'

She said airily: 'I don't like children.'

He thought of his son, and laughed. 'Well, they don't stay children!'

She seemed a child herself, of course, ageless. Yet he wondered if her naivety did not give her access to things which others missed, as if it were an innocent intelligence. She said: 'In Belgium I am an *infirmière à domicile*, a private nurse. I look after old people, Robert.'

He was pleased she spoke his name at last (she pronounced it 'Robber'). 'What do you do for them?'

'I dress their hurts . . . *jambes ulcérés*. Sometimes I bathe them.'

But instead of clarifying her, he thought, inquiry only made her more confusing. How could she devote herself to the old? She took their temperatures, helped them onto the lavatory, bathed their bodies. It must be like washing corpses. He hated age, feared it. But she mysteriously embraced it, even mimicked it in her body's unfruitfulness. He realised he was jealous of Louis; jealous even of those ancient, naked bodies. She had such beautiful hands. He said: 'You like working with the old.'

'Some of them are kind.'

'But they die on you.'

'Ah yes.' She smiled. 'One day I find Madame Rivoire sitting on her chair, quite upright. I suppose it was *la rigidité cadavérique*. Even her chin up like this.' She lifted her profile to him and closed her eyes.

For a moment he savoured the flow of her features down from the crushed cowlicks on her forehead, over the closed lashes stroking her cheeks, to the long, delicate jawline. She held this stance for what seemed a long time, so that it occurred to him that at last she was flirting. He wanted to kiss those full lips. They were fractionally parted. But the next moment her eyes were open again, and he heard his own voice, distracted, but carrying on: 'Was she very old?'

She said: 'But the old don't want to die either. They are often feared.'

'Often afraid.'

'Afraid, yes. Very much.'

Robert thought: people's lives are too long anyway. Why dedicate yourself to continuing them? He said: 'What made you train for a job like that?'

But she only answered: 'I think you are an intolerant man,' and her laughter sounded again.

Were his inquiries too uncouth, he wondered, too obvious? Or was this how she repulsed all male advances?

Her laughter ended every bout, like the bell in a boxing ring.

Suddenly she said: 'Will you write about our journey?'

He was taken aback. Did she suspect him of hunting down a story in her, searching for some angle? It was true, that familiar writer's impulse had been there at first: noting the language of her hands, memorising her verbal expressions, the way her eyebrows feathered upward at the ends. But for long minutes he had forgotten all this. She had made him forget.

She went on: 'What are you writing about, Robber?'

'Anything I can.' It seemed a bleak truth.

'So you will put me in?' Somewhere between a question and a statement. 'Yes, I am very interesting. Put me in.'

*So THERE she is. Josiane. Collected in a broken-backed notebook.*

*She rides very light, like a fairy. Those curious, violet eyes. Ridiculous contrast to Louis. He like a frog: puffy glands, wide mouth (talks too much), protuberant eyes. How did their union happen? How old is she, anyway? Twenty-five, perhaps. But could be eighteen or thirty.*

*Last night, very tired, found her feeding her horse stale croissants: from Louis's hard rations, I suppose. Followed her to the stream, where she was photographing lilies. She keeps me baffled. That full-stop laughter. 'I don't like children.' Tinkle. 'The horses feel nothing.' Tinkle. 'The old are feared.' (Maybe she meant that.)*

*Perhaps this is what happens with suppressed intelligence. It surfaces as simplicity.*

*But she holds everything at one remove, buffered. She dresses impotent bodies. She herself is a fashion plate. Louis looks like Balzac (she says). Lilies are memories.*

# Six

THE HIGHEST pass lay at 15,000 feet in shining snow. Around it the slabs and fangs of the Choquetecarpo mountains crossed the sky like the crenellations of a burnt-out city. A huge glacier was draped in their folds. Gazing behind him, Francisco imagined he saw the watershed of the Apurimac shining like a painted backdrop. But in fact they had left it behind long ago. The river bed they followed was icy and littered with boulders the size of houses. A light hail began to fall. They were entering the serried hulks of mountains they had never glimpsed before.

The pain in Francisco's feet – it would creep up, by the afternoon's end, to convulse half his body – had become his daily stigmata. He thought of it as the necessary price: his passport through this sacred Inca land. Through the lens of this pain, until recently, everything had seemed exalted. Only now had the mountains begun to empty his stomach – unless it was this cold dawn. Above him the granite peaks burst up like daggers. He felt them growing hostile. Their sanctity could not be his. He wondered about altitude sickness. Was it this apprehension? The trail was rutted with the stones of an Inca road, as if the group was being ushered on its way by these betrayed people. Soon they heard only the crunch of their feet and sticks in the snow. It was very still. They crossed the tracks of a puma.

And the muleteers: it was terrible to look at them, the conquered. Even at this height they bore loads on their backs as the animals did. And nobody noticed them. It was as if the conquistadors of Trujillo were riding alongside. *'They take two or three thousand Indians to serve them and carry their food and fodder, heavily loaded in shackles and dying of hunger. When Indians grew exhausted, they cut off their heads without untying them from their chains, leaving the road full of dead bodies, with the utmost cruelty.'*

These people, Francisco thought, were burdened into eternity, and he wondered why. Only two weeks ago he had witnessed a procession leaving a church in Lima. Its purpose was familiar – the bearing of Our Lady through the city – but it was pervaded by a peculiar melancholy. A wax Madonna, whose raiment splayed about her like fantastical wings, had come swaying out of the porch on a mahogany litter. Her cloak was sewn with cut glass and plastic fruit, and a silver-plated halo wobbled on her head. To Francisco she seemed a tawdry shadow of Our Lady of Victory in Trujillo. Her lifted hands were crusted in cheap rings.

But it was those who struggled to carry this monstrous weight – thirty or forty of them – who riveted his gaze: a religious fraternity dressed in Quechua bonnets. They had the raw cheekbones of their Inca ancestors, and looked racked by some inherited tragedy: Christ's Passion inextricable with their own. Under the towering litter they took shuffling, arthritic steps. Their low foreheads and full lips seemed rudely intensified, knotted and gasping with strain. From time to time they stopped to lay their burden down, only to heave it up again with the same fearful, tender anxiety, to the din of a discordant brass band.

Eerily they had reminded Francisco of something else; but only now did he realise what it was, and it turned him cold. It was something he had read in early chronicles, but seen only in his imagination: the litter of the sacred Inca Atahualpa borne peaceably towards his first meeting with the Spaniards among thousands of unarmed followers. '*Although the Spaniards killed the Indians who were carrying the litter, other replacements immediately went to support it. Many Indians had their hands cut off but continued to support their ruler with their shoulders . . . Atahualpa was captured in this way. Those who were carrying the litter and those who escorted the Inca never abandoned him: all died around him.*'

That litter had followed Francisco through boyhood in his mother's books: its fate pathetic, innocent, like the death of swarming bees.


As CAMILLA emerged from her tent, the moon was rising over the mountains. It turned the Inca steps to rumpled fish scales disintegrating into the valley. She hugged herself against the cold. She felt her whole body throb, but pleasurably, like something tested and secure. Only her calves were too tender.

She ran her hands over her roughened hair. Whimsically — perhaps because of this purging freshness of the night — she imagined herself slipping into a renewed skin, another self. Of course there was no other self: only these impulses named Camilla. Yet she felt on the brink of some unsought change, like the birth of a new capacity in a child, or a tide turning. It was impossible, of course, and strange.

After a while she noticed a figure ascending the stair. Yet she stayed where she was, with her fingers tangled in her hair, waiting. The figure was so small that she imagined it far away, but the man was quite close. He passed within a yard of her – an old Quechua farmer whose legs were bound in sacking. Where he was going in the moonlight, she could not imagine. But after a minute he turned back and stood shyly in front of her. The moon frosted his stubble. He said something she did not understand, then fumbled in his bag and handed her a potato. It was still warm from the fire.

'*Gracias.*'

'*Buenas noches, Señora.*'

She watched him disappear up the stairway of fish scales into the dark. She had an urge to follow him, she had no idea why. The potato felt soft and mealy between her teeth.

# Seven

IN 1537, with his empire crumbled behind him, the Inca ruler Manco, brother of Atahualpa, withdrew into the jungled mountains west of Vilcabamba. There he regrouped his depleted court in the hill fortress of Vitcos, and hoped to be left in peace.

Vitcos was abandoned now – the Spaniards had sacked it the same year – and the muleteers set up camp by a stream beneath its hill. A village had grown up in this wilderness, and for the first time the group felt respite. At dawn they found cattle grazing round their tents, and a pair of schoolgirls passed by, greeting them with a shy 'Caballeros, buenos días.'

When they climbed the hilltop ruins they did so at leisure, walking tenderly behind the guide, like cripples, at their own pace, until they came to an upland valley. It opened round them like a theatre under a thundery sky. They stopped on its edge. Even before the guide pointed, they saw the rock bursting like a bone from the grass. It was sudden and strange: a mountainous boulder of dark granite streaming with white lichen. It was as if the core of the earth were manifesting itself, and the hewn blocks scattered about signalled that the Inca had worshipped it.

As they approached they saw that its surface was carved with benches, altars, platforms. They clambered gingerly over it. Once, the guide said, it had been the holiest object in the refugee Inca state. But now the meaning of its carvings was unknown. They tried to follow the channels wriggling over its face – gutters which had flowed with sacrificial beer or llama blood – but the grooves tapered into confusion. They climbed steps which no longer led to anything. All round the giant boulder, lesser ones had been sculpted into the appearance of thrones or troughs, but their function was lost. They looked interchangeable. Everything had returned to pure shape, its human purpose gone.

Robert told what little he knew. But Camilla was aware of the new fatigue in him, and guessed his frustration at all this incoherence.

He himself heard his voice as little more than a series of distrustful echoes, as if words had fallen out of use as tools to describe anything. No wonder the Inca refused to write them. Instead they had found this language of untranslated stone.

'There was supposed to be a spirit living in the rock.' His foot tapped on its surface. 'It was once surrounded by temples.' Below its far edge, where it fell sheer, a sombre pool shone between stone foundations. 'The spirit rose from the water. People even saw it. The Spaniards called it a demon and said it threatened people to worship it and feed it silver. In the end they burnt the temples down.'

Francisco said softly: 'The Inca practised idolatry.' This was certain, whatever his own people's sins.

They all stared down twenty feet into the water. Francisco hated the presence of these others, except for Camilla. He felt they were defiling the place. But defiling what? Josiane was at his elbow, with her doll's face, like a decadent child, confusing him. She smelt of church.

Robert said: 'You Spaniards denied the Inca their god.' He felt irritated by the way Francisco gazed at Camilla with those calf's eyes. He went on: 'The Spanish branded all Inca gods as devils. They just replaced one primitive belief with another.'

There was silence. The pool shone back at them. Francisco, standing between Louis and Josiane, looked down in a turmoil of embarrassment and anger.

Josiane said: 'Maybe it was a demon. Maybe it's still here.'

In this desanctified place, under the louring sky, the child-like voice seemed to propose a possibility. For several minutes Robert had been conscious of her beside him as a delicate, sexual presence. Now he felt obscurely disconcerted. He said sharply: 'What do you mean, a demon?'

'Something evil.'

Francisco raised his eyes to her, then down to the water again. Did she know what she meant? The water was no more than a smeared mirror of rain over a floor of grass, but it was dimmed by shifting lights – the effect of clouds – and was unfathomable now. Their reflected heads wavered above the lip of the rock. Often, he thought, the Inca must have looked down as he did and wondered: Who is it? Do I somehow exist inside those waters? Down there, in the hinterland behind the surface, what becomes of me? Or is it some other being? Vertically below them,

73

the boulder was carved with steps descending to the pool. The steps disappeared under the reflected sheen of the sky. The Inca, watching them, must have known that at any moment the demon might break through the surface into common day.

Francisco went on smarting under Robert's words. He imagined Camilla wanting to say something, but her head was averted. She would not contradict her husband.

Robert was saying: 'The voice of the conquered always goes unheard, doesn't it?' He sounded bitter even to himself. It was this Inca voice which he had longed to recover. But it was echoing fainter all the time.

Francisco peered into the pool again. He wondered if the devil might still inhabit it. Had his people so flouted God that He had denied them the power to destroy demons? He wished he could ask his confessor. His head shimmered back at him in an opaque circle. He could not see his features. They might be those of anyone, anything. He felt faint vertigo.

'Demons? Demons, well, why not?' It was Louis's voice, rumbling and jocular. 'Demons give a place cachet. *Ils vous forcent de rester alerte.*' He grasped Josiane's shoulder. 'Why do people always accept heaven and dismiss hell? Wish-fulfilment! For myself, I fulfil a wish for demons!' He flung out a summoning arm over the water, and as his laughter volleyed out, the others realised how long it was since they had heard it. It rolled with an earthy confidence, restored a sense of proportion. 'Demons arise!' Even Francisco felt relieved, as if this man had exorcised something.

Louis's laughter went on sounding in his own head. Weariness, he thought, was extinguishing all their sense of

74

judgement and humour. As for a demon, he imagined some frogman-priest rising up those tell-tale steps by torchlight, and commanding the worshippers to surrender their trinkets. A holy scam of near-Christian cunning. He began to warm to the Inca.

Later, from a platform at the top of the steps, Robert too imagined the invocation of the water-demon, of Josiane's evil. A brackish smell rose from the sodden grass. Evil, he thought, was just a word for anything repellent that people did not understand. A faint wind furrowed the water between the stones. At night, he thought, like many Inca pools, it would have become an observatory where the stars were studied in reflection. The water contained the sky, and so became holy. The stars, after all, were gods. In the pool they descended to vivify the world of men. Even the dead came down. At the winter solstice, they crossed the Milky Way, as over a white bridge, and touched earth again. A primeval fancy, of course. But he imagined his parents walking the Milky Way, his father with his shooting stick, scowling, his mother leading her dalmatians. He must be weak, he thought, physically weak, because his eyes were pricking. His father had been dead twelve years.

He wanted to leave here now. There was nothing else to see. Just these stone shapes whose purpose had abandoned them. He couldn't be sure what anything was. Nobody had recorded it. It had no voice.

ON THE crest of the hill he came to Manco's palace. Its walls had crumbled into ridges and mounds where towers

75

jutted, and a herdsman was grazing his cows in the overgrown court.

Robert identified the rooms without feeling. There was no one, in any case, to listen to whatever he might have known. The others had dispersed through the ruins. With dulled surprise he remembered his passion of a few days before in the hill-citadel of Choquequirau. He might have been looking back on a remote time. But the familiar hallmarks were all in place – the Inca door jambs and monolithic lintels – and a few gates stood complete in the hewn strength of their stone. He pressed his hands over the ashlars of a sunk window, resting his palms on their warmth, hoping their touch would revive him. But because he could not capture the buildings in words, they seemed to exist less. The stone felt carved too long ago. It was stained with dead lichen.

Following a sunken way, he came face to face with Josiane. She was hugging her shoulders, although the wind had dropped and a filtered sunlight shone. She said: 'You were very unkind to Francisco.'

'Did you believe that stuff about a demon?'

'I don't know. Maybe.'

He stared at her. She, with this whole country, was withdrawing behind a veil which emitted only codes. He said almost angrily: 'You must know what you believe.' They were walking side by side.

'No.'

'So you think evil is specific, like a disease. Perhaps you think the Inca were evil.'

She laughed: her silvery, confusing sound. It was impossible to tell if it was mocking or empty. 'I think the Inca were very small.'

'What?'

'The gates are very low. Mountain people. Like mine in the Midi. They don't grow.'

She hugged herself again, shivered. He noticed a faint flush along her cheeks. He said: 'Are you well?'

'I don't know. I'm not cold, I'm hot.'

'Perhaps you should go back to the camp.' He touched her arm. 'It's been too hard a journey.'

'Oh no.'

He realised he had spoken only for himself. She looked animated, even happy. This single day – an oasis in their ordeal – was returning the others to wellbeing.

She said: 'We're only four days from Vilcabamba.'

He said: 'It had better be worth it.'

'The guide thinks it won't, he says it's overgrown. But Louis says only Europeans understand ruins. I think it will be wonderful, Vilcabamba.'

Robert could not answer. Vilcabamba still seemed less a place than an idea. And when they arrived, it might mean no more than these grey gates and foundations, from which the mana had gone. Now, walking beside this woman over the indecipherable stones, their elusiveness only made him tired. Simultaneously she roused and disappointed him.

Her eyes were glittering: they were too bright. Some sadness in his own words caught him unawares as he said: 'You must find Louis.' At this moment which she would not even recognise, he realised that he was releasing her – or releasing himself, consciously laying aside whatever he had felt for her, like a suit which didn't fit.

'Louis will be sleeping somewhere.' She laughed and

wandered blithely away. 'He says it is too great a sacrifice to walk today. It is like working on a Sunday.'

ROBERT LAY down on the edge of the palace square, feeling a confused regret. For a minute he heard her sandals slapping over the compacted earth. Then nothing. The grass spread soft under his back. Here, while Manco was playing quoits with Spanish renegades to whom he had given sanctuary, they murdered him in cold blood. Camilla came in silence and sat nearby. The slopes and summits of jungled hills pressed round in a dark circle.

After a while, from somewhere they could not locate, they heard the tremble of an Andean flute. It was an unmistakable sound. They had heard it once before, in a town of northern Italy, and had emerged into the square to find a troupe of Peruvian Indians busking there, isolated in this ancient city of another land. They were making a heartrending music on flutes and drums, and were dancing in a circle with their heads down, round and round, oblivious to the tourists snapping them. And now this music rose again, breathy and thinned: a single Quechua flute far out in the hills. To Robert's ear it was lamenting everything lost, and perhaps forgotten, by these orphaned people: a plangent leftover severed from its origins. Neither he nor Camilla stirred to find its source. They only smiled at one another and closed their eyes again, until the sound died with the same throaty abruptness as it had started.

He did not know how much time had passed before he heard the brushing of someone's feet over the grass, and a voice murmured '*Señor!*'

Robert opened his eyes on a man he had not seen

before. He was a *mestizo* herdsman, his jacket chafed thin by the rope slung over his shoulders. He had dark, shy eyes. '*Le interesan las cosas viejas?*' He was holding out something between the tips of his fingers.

Grudgingly Robert got to his feet and accepted it. A fragment of discoloured cotton lay brittle on his palm. Woven into the fabric he saw a fabulous beast – a jaguar, perhaps – in crimson and faded blue.

'Where does this come from?'

'*Treinta soles.*'

'No. Where from?' He gestured at the land. '*Donde?*'

The man looked back at him regretfully, as if he had breached some private decorum, then dropped his gaze. He said: '*Una momia*' and tenderly took the fragment back.

Camilla had stood up too. 'What is it?'

'It's a piece of mummy wrapping.' Robert turned back to the man. '*Momia. Donde?*'

The man looked round him, then gestured loosely across the slope. '*Allá!*' But his fist had closed over the cotton scrap, and he did not move.

Robert beckoned Camilla to his side.

'Please show us?' He motioned to where the herdsman had pointed.

He was not sure if the man had understood, but they followed him as he tramped through the wrecked guard-posts of the palace and along a scrub-covered spur. After a while his walk turned into a furtive lope, and once or twice he turned to check that they were following.

Robert warned himself: this is ridiculous. There are no Inca mummies here. The Spanish destroyed the last ones. The man's a charlatan. But he told himself this to quell the excitement spreading in him, and to stop his heart pounding. Because that woven rag must have come from somewhere. His footsteps were light and shaky at the man's heels, and his eyes scarcely left his back. He had an idea the herdsman might evaporate like a genie. Once, looking up at the ruined palace, he saw a silhouette moving over the terraces, and recognised the fastidious gait of Josiane. She stopped to sit down on a pile of rubble and stared into the air above them.

Just where a shelf of rock overhung their way, they came to a rough-hewn wall against the cliff. Through its entrance they stooped into a cramped chamber mottled with sunlight. Its air was warm and dry. The herdsman had his back to them, but when he stood aside they saw a figure hunched on the stone ledge beyond him. For a moment, so naturally was it sitting, they imagined it alive. Then they saw that the yellow knees and head stuck through a carapace of discoloured cloth. The skin gleamed like polished wood and had broken apart over the body's joints to show knobs of amber-coloured bone. The herdsman stood beside it, as if by something he had committed, and watched them. He had a broad, simple face, but his eyes kept shifting. And the figure, when they looked more closely, was shocking. It seemed to be a man still young, his knees drawn to his chin, his scalp matted in black hair, even his eyelashes intact. Out of his rotted wrappings curled a pair of desiccated arms. The fingers were linked with knotted twine, separately, and splayed rigid over his closed eyes. Either at the moment of death, or in a feared future, he seemed to be cringing from something unspeakable.

Camilla whispered: 'What have they done to him?'

'I don't know. Sometimes they heated or smoked them. Sometimes the corpses just mummified in the air.'

She said: 'We shouldn't be here.'

Robert was stooping over the naked shoulders. 'Of course we should. It's extraordinary. There's nothing sacred about it. There are hundreds of mummies in museums.'

'This is different.'

At that moment the herdsman lifted the figure — it seemed light as eiderdown — and placed it in the fuller light near the entrance. '*Quiere un pedacito?*' He started to tear off a piece of bandage.

'Stop, stop. No!' Camilla blazed at him.

'It doesn't matter.' Robert knelt to scrutinise the wrappings. He wondered if the designs — a stylised interplay of men and beasts — might harbour the complexity of a script. But their continuity was lost in the clefts of the body. He said: 'It was a custom of some cultures to mummify like this. It only looks odd . . .'

'It's private.'

'It's not private.' He was growing irritated. 'The Inca paraded their mummies in state.' He kept his back to her. He wanted her just to shut up while he absorbed this find: the sheer luck of it. He said: 'The Inca treated their mummies as living beings. They chatted to them, sometimes ate with them, even used them as entitlements to land.'

'But we're strangers here.' She looked down at the yellowed, blinding hands. 'We're intruders.'

But Robert was not listening. He had plucked out his notebook and was writing furiously.

She went on: 'Anyway, they're not living. They're

dead. They've been dead for hundreds of years. They deserve peace.'

'Of course they're dead.' Robert's gaze flickered between the corpse and his notepad. 'Only the Inca imagined they conversed with them.' His voice had turned harsh. 'That's not consoling, is it? That immortality consists of preservation in the memory of others.'

She recognised an angry grief in him. Years ago, hunting to comfort him after his father's death, she had offered him the same forlorn cliché: eternity in people's remembrance. Even then he had rejected it, while unhappily embracing her.

Now, as if reading her thought, he said: 'Because memories are never quite true, are they? The real self gets stopped for ever. The Inca didn't interact with the dead. They were just left with projections and misunderstandings.' He twisted the mummy more fully towards him. 'There's nobody here. He isn't here.' Then he started writing again, fast, afraid that the herdsman was going to evict them before he had noted all the cadaver's details.

Camilla turned her back on him. The scribble of his pen nauseated her. Every time he completed a page it made a self-satisfied crackle. She glanced at the herdsman, seeking support, but he did not comprehend. He only wrenched at his hat in his hands, nursing some shame of his own. In the end she steadied her voice and said to the wall: 'I think the dead deserve the same privacy as people who are ill or asleep. They're defenceless.'

Robert went on writing. 'You said yourself they were *dead.*'

'Our bodies are important.'

'These are scarcely even bodies. They've been eviscera ted.'

She peered down again at the cringing man. She realised she was shaking, shaking with something like pity. She even wanted to take the young man in her arms. She could see no incisions on his shrivelled torso. She only said: 'He's still a person.'

'No. There's nothing there. No heart, liver, not even brain fluids. They drained them out.'

Even as Robert spoke – and his own words sounded separate from him, more unsparing – he felt the strangeness of it. He was looking down on an embalmed husk. All the internal organs of such corpses had been extracted through the anus or vagina, leaving only these airy shadows. To the Inca, it seemed, it was the outer, not the inner, which carried deepest meaning: the appearances encountered day by day. In embalmment even the brain – the seat of memory – trickled down as liquid through the body, to be absorbed by the cotton pad on which the corpse sat. So everything a person was, his whole remembered past, became condensed to a cotton tampon. Robert glanced about the rock chamber, as if there might be something else. But it was bare. He thought: in the dried fluids of the dead brain are all the human stories there have ever been. And he imagined them released into the air at death – the memories of all the past, of the Inca, of his father – flying free on some stratum of their own: the whole air clamouring with stories.

But Camilla had stepped angrily away from the corpse. She said: 'If he's nothing, why write about him? Leave him, leave him.' She had always hated this use of other people's tragedy, other people's sanctities. She recognised it only as a journalistic passion for sensation – a passion he claimed to despise.

She walked out into the sunlight and stared at the hills. The macabre made good copy, of course. But as her anger cooled she realised, with faint shame, that it was not really the violation which repelled her. In her work as a private researcher, after all, she was a collector of facts. And if Robert could have created something from this apparition of grief, privacy, terror – whatever it was – she would have been glad. But she understood suddenly that he could not. He did not have that gift. She thought this with muted surprise and dismay. He could not do the dead man justice. And he did not even know.

She glanced back through the entrance behind her, but swung her gaze away again. Robert looked so arrogant standing there, noting this, detailing that, while the youth's hands shielded his dead eyes from the mad scribble. Robert would call her sentimental, of course, and it was true she was as fraudulent as he. A faithful description, however intrusive, would have moved her. But long before they started on this journey, she realised, she had been afraid.

Not that Robert was second-rate: in his way he was extraordinary. He could conjure with ideas and deploy facts out of his retentive memory. But he could not describe a face or a feeling. This talent, she supposed, had little to do with intellect or even empathy. It was just a gift, or even an aberration, like ingrowing toenails. And there were too many things he simply did not notice (sometimes she felt herself among them) or perhaps did not think worth his attention.

But as Robert stooped out of the rock tomb, the halo of

achievement which she expected whenever he pocketed a replete notebook was vitiated by something else in him, almost sorrowful. Behind him the herdsman was fingering a tip, but had sold nothing. And Camilla felt perverse disappointment. Robert no longer looked quite himself – his confidence seemed edged with apprehension – and her anger was draining away.

THAT EVENING a great storm broke over the mountains. Batteries of lightning lit the camp for minutes on end, as if somebody had barged inside the tents with a flash-camera, and a heavy, unseasonal rain fell for six hours.

Francisco could not read for more than a few minutes at a time. His candle kept guttering out, and his hands shook whenever it thundered. Once a muleteer looked in, and with the odd tenderness of these men, asked if he was well. The Señora Josiane, the man said, had fallen ill. But Francisco did not know what to do about this. He felt the Belgians despised him. Tonight he did not even go to the supper-tent, but folded away his books and unwrapped his Inca mirror like a talisman.

The rain deepened to a hard drumming over the canvas. He let the candle gutter out and lay in his sleeping-bag under the strobic lightning-flashes, rubbing the quartz with his shirtsleeve. He was conscious of holding it more delicately than before. Back in Spain it had seemed sterilised in its exile, and somehow long past. But now, when he turned it in his hands, it looked unfamiliar. He had the idea that its native mountains and cities had recharged it with an old power. The opaque sheen of its stone had turned baleful. His people had stolen it, after all. His face no longer belonged there.

LOUIS WAS not alarmed by Josiane's fever. The girl was delicate. In Hainaut she would sometimes complain of a mild malaise or headache, and whatever influenza was going round would be sure to lodge itself in that frail organism.

But her discomfort made him lose his temper with this whole imbecile expedition. They had sought a riding holiday away from the backpackers of Cuzco, and instead had blundered into this purgatory, where they were being travestied by a British journalist and prayed for by a Spanish priest. It would take a month in Paris or Provence to recover.

Josiane was lying on her sleeping-bag under the pounding canvas, the flush darkened on her cheeks. Back in Belgium he would have dropped into fatherly concern, cooking her a little plain fish or a herb omelette and by morning she would have recovered. They both enjoyed these roles – her fragility seemed to counterbalance his middle age. But here they were reduced to the unspeakable Quechua cuisine. She would have to recover on dust-dry jungle potatoes, yams, tinned milk, dried chicken, banana, papaya.

He wondered angrily how he had let this happen. How many days were left? Four? Five? And Vilcabamba, he thought. We are all dreaming of Vilcabamba! He stretched out sweating beside Josiane. It didn't take much to know what Vilcabamba would be like. It carried the spurious glamour of defeat. Nobody dared admit it, he thought, but the Inca were boring. They were ruled by a dreary, mechanistic communism, brightened only by an emperor who pretended he spoke to the sun. With their roads and laws and dearth of civilised pleasures, they were the Romans of the early American world.

He thought: even these ruined cities, whatever the Englishman says, are architecturally null. Their doors and niches scream out for an arch. But the Inca never invented one. Their palaces were overgrown cottages. They never imagined the dome or played with the squinch. They had no wheel, no lathe, no iron. And these people were coeval with the Medici! Wander their rectangular ruins for an hour and you came out masturbating, dreaming of curves, and marvelling at the undiscovered miracle of the keystone.

It was the same with all unimaginative people, he thought, including his old partners in Hainaut. They couldn't translate between forms. So they mouldered in a rut and called themselves purists. The Inca, like them, were the stuff of soldiers, administrators, farmers: dull, worthy folk. As for Atahualpa, you'd scarcely invite him to dinner. When Pizarro came across him, he'd just drunk corn beer from his brother's skull, and used his skin as a tom-tom.

Every time Josiane winced at the thunder, he pulled her silk nightdress closer against her chin, and felt a rankling helplessness. Nothing in this expedition, he realised, had given him pleasure. He had felt himself turn elderly. Exhaustion had descended less like muscular fatigue than an innate weariness. Once or twice he had even imagined another self – somebody slim and dapper – riding in front of him on another horse. This self had once existed – he had seen him in photographs – but he was out of date. The river of time did not take you evenly, no. You woke up wrinkled one morning at the foot of some rapids,

87

At some stage during the past few years this slender man had been usurped by a portly Sancho Panza on a gasping horse. It had not taken long.

Occasionally, too, he imagined himself in the eyes of the others: a comfortable hedonist. He might have kept a certain dignity alone, even on horseback. Instead he was being driven by love of a young wife to ape a man half his age. Was anyone laughing? By every noon, exertion had discoloured his face and the hair under his fedora was like damp porridge. He could feel the sag of his own hips. Not that he felt the need to impress anyone here – or anyone anywhere – but for himself sometimes, and for Josiane, he wished for his youth's energy back, and that his Rubens body looked less celebratory.

After a while, as he was wondering whether to go to supper, the tent flap opened on Camilla. The rain was streaming down her face. She was carrying some pills to reduce fever, and her expression was arranged into a concern she did not much feel.

Josiane turned on her sleeping-bag and murmured: 'Thank you,' and then: 'Stay a moment. Stay, will you?'

Camilla looked at Louis. 'You go and eat. I'll stay with her.'

Louis took the pills, and warmed a little to this dull woman. He touched his wife's hand – 'I won't be long' – then pushed out into the storm.

INSIDE THE tent a pair of Calor gas-lamps shed a cold glare. The rain was falling with a dense, leaden warmth. Camilla stood awkwardly for a moment before this sickly orna-ment of a girl – even in bed Josiane looked manufactured. She was cushioned among her own clothes, and her wide-open eyes and the crimson ovals on her cheeks heightened the illusion of a brittle doll. Around her Camilla noticed a scattering of unshared luxuries: *petit four* biscuits, Medjool dates, some bottles of Armagnac and Chartreuse. She bunched up Louis's sleeping-bag and knelt against it, then touched the back of her hand to Josiane's forehead. It was clammy. 'Do you still feel hot?'

'Cold now. I shiver.' Her voice had gone dry, its accent harsh.

'You have a thermometer?'

'No. Maybe the guide owns one.' She smiled: a vacant smile, Camilla thought, inviting nothing. 'I do not worry. I get these sometimes.'

'Fevers?'

'Nausea. I get it from anything. Some kinds of flowers, food, some kinds of situations.'

'What kind of situations?'

'I don't know in English. When things go wrong.'

Poor Louis, Camilla thought.

Josiane closed her eyes, but her pillowed profile was held too self-consciously for sleep. Camilla watched the flushed symmetry of her face, and for an instant envied the delicacy which she herself had never had. But the next moment she was thinking: if it's possible to be both beautiful and vacuous, the model is here.

Once she sensed Josiane tremble faintly all through her body. 'Do you need a blanket?' She dissolved some aspirin into a cup of water and held it to her lips. 'This can't harm you.' But her own tenderness grated on her. She felt trapped in her gender, in the nurse's forced role of caring. She found a blanket and laid it over the girl's legs. Josiane struck her as ridiculous, with her nineteenth-century pouts and primness and her spoilt child's voice. The air reeked of her scent.

She lowered her own forehead to Josiane's: it felt moist, cold. She's probably hypochondriac, Camilla thought, but this fever is real. Yet the guide had said that malaria and typhus were unknown in these hills. Could it be psychosomatic? Situations, she had said. Camilla began, not knowing: 'You can't get fever from stress. In any case, there are no "situations" here, are there? Not between us? And you're happy with Louis.' She felt she was speaking to a baby. 'Unless the whole journey . . .'

Josiane did not open her eyes. 'No. *Louis est le meilleur des maris*. And everything. I have not to worry. Francisco, too. And your Robert. He is very nice, very *attentif* . . .'

'Is he?' Camilla did not know if the word contained some nuance in French.

'Yes, and he is excited by everything, I think. He is not like an Englishman, is he?'

Camilla did not know what to make of this. 'No, not very.' She wondered what Robert had seen in Josiane, other than her fey prettiness, then she thought: of course, that is enough.

Josiane's eyes opened. They looked too shining. 'He is writing about our journey, isn't he? He said he would put me in.' She propped herself on her elbows. 'Have you seen my mirror?'

Camilla placed Josiane's handbag on her lap, and waited while she studied herself in the little glass, patting her semicircle of cowlicks and touching lipstick to her mouth.

Camilla watched with deepening distaste. Where did the woman imagine she was? The rain was still beating on the canvas and the thunder exploding from end to end of the dark. Camilla thought: I have no compassion, not a drop. I would not care if this woman died tonight. Maybe that's what this feeling of change in me really is. Not an evolution at all; but a cutting off, a casting free.

At last Josiane laid aside her mirror with a small smile. Her flush was fading. She seemed satisfied that she had maintained the person she wanted to be, or the person Louis wanted. She said out of the blue: 'Camilla, do you have children?'

'I have a son.'

'Ah.'

Josiane was silent for so long that Camilla thought she could ask: 'And you, would you like children?'

'Oh no. That would change too much.'

'Yes, children change everything.' But Camilla wondered what Josiane meant. What would change? Her body, merely, or Louis, or her own childish role.

Camilla added, too brightly, because her son seemed farther away than he had ever been: 'Safer to be single like Francisco!'

But she had wanted a second child.

Josiane gave her dry laugh. 'Poor Francisco.'

'Well, that's what he's chosen.'

'But does Robert mind?'

'Robert?'

'How Francisco looks at you. He has cow's eyes.'

Was it so obvious? Camilla thought. 'I don't suppose Robert has even noticed.' But Josiane had. How strange.

'Robert was hard to him.'

Camilla said: 'It's not personal. He's hard on facts and ideas, not on people.' But she wondered.

The next moment Louis clambered cursing on all fours into the tent.

'Good God, we were offered quinao soup and bananas again! I'm turning into a banana.'

He stooped to kiss Josiane. 'Do I smell like a banana? Have I become a banana republic?'

He looked so comical, with a drop of rain on his nose, that Camilla burst out laughing.

He asked: 'How is she?'

'I think the fever's going.'

Josiane said: 'I can't eat.' Her voice had turned petulant.

Louis laughed, 'You're lucky!', but he bent down and caressed her head.

She said: 'Am I very pale?'

But she knew exactly how she looked, Camilla thought. She had dabbed blusher along her cheeks a moment ago. Perhaps Josiane did not even recognise her infantile persona, she had used it so long.

So Camilla said goodnight and went out into the dark. For a luxurious minute she stood immune in the rain as it pelted down on her head and anorak and watertight boots, and looked across to her tent, where Robert's shadow crouched in an illumined pyramid. A blitz of lightning whitened the boulders and scrub as she started to walk.

She thought: was this what it meant to be a woman, even now? To mask yourself in paints? To look and smell differently from how you looked and smelt? Perhaps it was a symptom of Robert's cooling towards her − or hers to him − that she no longer spent hours at the hair stylist or choosing a dress. Even now she might have thrown off her hood and let the rain bedraggle her. But no, she had not grown indifferent to how she looked. She simply preferred to look another way. Often lately she had dressed for her own eyes, to feel at ease with herself. She supposed she had always valued simplicity. Her clothes were austere (her friends said), she disliked jewellery. She had decided that the wrinkles edging her eyes were part of her personality.

Perhaps she was simply growing selfish.

# *Eight*

FRANCISCO KNELT in a pew of the mission church, and prayed for the remission of sins. Outside, little but a ruined belfry remained from the silver-mining town of San Francisco de la Victoria, which the Spanish had founded four centuries ago, even as the conquered Vilcabamba was sinking back into jungle forty miles away. At first he could hear only the barking of the mission dogs, but later, after the tapping of feet in the porch, he imagined the arrival of Camilla behind him, and the still-pale presence of Josiane. He dropped his head into his hands and prayed without thinking in a hoarse whisper out of his memory. *'Have pity and mercy upon all men whom thou hast made. Make them and their children to walk in a straight road, without thinking any evil. Grant that they may have a long life, and not die in their youth, and that they may live and feed in peace.'*

He knew it was not a Christian prayer. It was an Inca one, memorised from years back. But he let its whispered words rest in the Christian air. When he turned round again, Camilla and Josiane were gone. Perhaps they had never been there. The sun was leaking through the deep windows.

He rested his gaze on the altar. That morning they had trekked four hours from Vitcos and already his body was aching. His clasped hands – blistered by the bamboo poles – chafed against his cheeks. He wanted to sleep. After a while he discerned beside the altar a statue familiar from the churches of his home province: St James the Greater, his sword-arm raised, riding his charger over a prostrate Moor. He stared at it with old affection. But now, when he scrutinised the shape beneath, he saw that in place of the turbaned Moor struggled a pathetic figure in a woollen cap. It was the pagan Inca.

He averted his eyes. Was it a sin to pity the victim of a saint? His hands were wrenching against his face. But they were not saints who had trampled the Inca underfoot. They were his ancestors. The altar was banked with unlit candles, but he could not light one. His fingers had turned cold. Slowly he got up and went to the door. Beyond its porch was a clear sky. The ruined tower lifted two bells into empty space.

In the doorway he collided with the *mestizo* guide. In all these days they had scarcely exchanged a word, but now the man's face loomed a foot from his – a dark, glittering alloy of Spanish and Inca, forty years old maybe, swept by coarse black hair and an expression he could not read. As Francisco stepped aside for him to enter, the *mestizo*'s face set up a vague tension in him. The man smiled faintly, peremptorily, as he passed, and Francisco blurted: *Dios le bendiga!*'

He turned and saw the man stare up blankly at the altar. For a moment Francisco focused the aquiline Spanish nose and broad Quechua cheekbones, the blood of victor and victim flowing side by side. How could the man endure it? How did he manage to live at all, to bear the fragmentation in his soul? With a diffused guilt Francisco saw him lift one hand to the altar in the ancient Inca attitude of prayer, then bow and cross himself.

ROBERT COULD not later recall precisely when it dawned on him that Camilla was gone. At some time they had crossed a pass into the watershed of the Rio Pampaconas, and descended over steep grasslands. Far beneath them the river wound into forest under spurs of mountain, and a faint mist lifted from half the valleys, as if they were on fire. The air had turned humid. Then little by little the sunlight had dimmed, until they found themselves wending through a translucent fog high above the river. The guide and cook had gone ahead, Francisco with them, and Louis and Josiane – she rather silent now – were riding their horses along the track in front.

Then Robert realised that Camilla had dropped far behind. A few minutes before, it seemed, she had been admiring some *chilka* trees beside him. Now she had vanished. He stared down the path by which they had come. He could see a full hundred yards. The track wavered empty along the mountain precipice, no wider than a person, and beneath it, for hundreds of feet, was only misted air. He started down it, shaking. He did not dare to run – because every few yards opened up a new void. Between the track and the chasm was only a foot-wide fringe of bamboo and shrub which would never hold a footfall: it was a green trap-door into nothing.

He tried to peer over the edge. There was no noise but

the soughing of the river over its rocks. She had gone without a rustle or a cry. In the rarified air he tried to believe himself dreaming; the utterness of her absence was like hallucination. Then the cold air rushed up in his stomach.

*Days and months go by and we don't really speak together because we are always there. I wear her like a vest against my skin, unconsciously . . .*

Then he started to run down the track, and his running frightened him. It made no sound. He might have been bodiless. He shouted, 'Camilla!' But his voice was a harsh squeak. He shouted her name then, again and again, to fill up the air, the silence.

*This is the image that comes. A dinner table surrounded by people. The talk is of bereavement. They say you should not speak ill of the dead. I say such sanitised dead are not truly remembered; they stiffen into perfect masks, and die again. Camilla's is the face which says: I understand.*

Everything shook under him. Some great binding force had broken and seemed to be propelling him into an unthinkable future. After a minute he did not dare cry out her name any more. Its sound was breaking him inside. The moment her name died he was overwhelmed by unspeakable loneliness. He ran on, but wildly, kicking stones and earth in front of him, gasping aloud.

She was sitting behind a boulder, very white.

She had thought the mat of earth solid as she stepped to one side of the track. But her right leg had dropped through into nothing. For a second she had remained suspended, her body held in a cradle of shrubs and bamboo, her leg dangling. She had heard the foliage tearing under her back – then her fingers had closed around a tussock of *ichu* grass, which did not yield, and there was nothing left to fear.

Resting on her elbows above space, suspended, she had let her heartbeat subside. The river coiled far below her. High above, a flock of migrating ibis were flying north. For what seemed a long time she had rested on the shelf between earth and air, while her breathing stilled. When she started to heave herself up, curious to see if she could, she was surprised by the way her knees found purchase in the undergrowth, and how easily she crawled back onto the path.

She began softly to laugh, not in hysteria, just in mystification at being alive. Her hands trembled over her stomach, breasts. The commonplace is true, she thought: how close death always is. Stray off the path, the kerb, and you are gone. For days now they had been walking along oblivion.

She leant back against the rock, kneading the earth in her hands. It was dry with powdered leaves. She did not think about anything, but lay there for some minutes, and at last knotted her broken bootlace. The sun was warm.

She noticed Robert before he saw her. He was plunging down the track with his arms flailing like a boxer's. His eyes looked blind. When he saw her he stopped and let out a sobbing name. Then he was kneading her in his arms, as she recognised she had kneaded the earth, to confirm its texture, to know it existed. And she felt with surprise her own separateness. It was as if either her vision had blurred, or Robert had faded. He cupped her cheeks and lifted her face to his. But he looked so peculiar, with his mouth open and his hair adrift, that she found herself laughing. 'Robert, you look terrible!'

He felt her tense and resistant in his embrace. She went on laughing. He was still clasping her shoulders, feeling their firmness, her life, while bewilderment rose in him.

She said: 'Did you come down here for me?'

'Of course . . . I couldn't find you . . .'

'I was just resting.'

'Resting?'

'Yes. I put my foot through the foliage over there' – she gestured behind her – 'and broke a bootlace. I didn't know you'd be worried.'

'Well I was.' He embraced her again, but it felt awkward, and he sensed her like tautening rope, and at last pulled away. 'We'd better go on.'

He had violated some privacy in her, he knew. He did not understand it. This country changed people, even Camilla. It was changing him too, and all of them.

# Nine

'THEY ARE not gone, not really. Even now somebody will be walking over the earth near Cuzco and put his foot into a grave. The whole earth must be hollow with them, the dead. And their *apus*, the mountain gods, are still there, and the spirits in the rocks, like the stone at Vitcos which the Belgian laughed at.'

The guide did not often talk so much. Perhaps the sweet beer had mellowed him; and the night was soft round the candlelit tent, and only the English couple were left, with the Quechua cook hunched over his burner.

At first Robert felt they should not have mentioned the mummy. The *mestizo* had looked incensed, as if something had been vouchsafed them which by right was his. Now he said: 'I don't know what sort of mummy this was you saw. I've never heard of them at Vitcos. Maybe it came from another place. Maybe he was not Inca at all, but somebody else.'

Robert said: 'It was in a tomb.'

'It is bad luck to see them.' The guide still looked angry. 'I heard of a man near Pisac who fell into a grave where a mummy sat. He went mad. In the end a local shaman took skin from the mummy's finger and fed it to him, and he recovered. But these bodies are very scarce. Perhaps only the shamans know where they are. The herdsman who showed you this did wrong.'

Camilla could not meet the guide's gaze.

But Robert was scrutinising him, fascinated and surprised by his anger. He said: 'The man was trying to sell pieces of its wrappings. We refused.'

'He was evil.'

They were silent. The herdsman had seemed only gauche and ashamed, Robert thought.

After a while the guide gestured silently at the cook, who was sitting with his back to them, drinking the dregs of the soup. 'These Quechua people have forgotten their history,' he said. 'They don't know why they do things or how long their past is. But they still make gifts to the mountain gods. In my village is a very old shaman, who knows what every *apu* wants in season. How much maize, how much coca, perhaps an ornament. These are burnt facing the god.'

Robert listened without surprise. The Spaniards had never dissolved this shadow-world. And it was from Vilcabamba, in its brief day, that the natives had imagined the Inca past would return. Now it lingered like a memory-trace just beneath the Christian surface: even in the guide. The man's pragmatism seemed to be slipping from him. His face had turned restless.

He said: 'The mountain gods watch the llama flocks especially. I've seen men sacrifice their finest animal, facing the peak, and pull out its heart still beating and smear the blood over the rest of the flock to protect them.'

His eyes flickered between them, checking for disbelief. 'Sometimes I think our past is angry with us.'

'Angry?' Camilla was frowning.

'Because we have neglected the ancestors, the Oldest Ones. I don't mean our fathers' fathers, or their fathers. I mean the *Ñaupa Machu*, who lived even before the oldest, before time.' It no longer occurred to him that he might be disbelieved. 'You can often hear them in the mountain clefts and mines, talking in the dark. They can be very terrible. Sometimes they can eat a person up, slowly.'

'No,' Camilla whispered without thinking.

But the guide did not even hear.

By day, with his digital watch and baseball cap, he appeared Spanish and rather urban, Robert thought; but in this evening's candlelight, with a woollen cap tugged close round his narrow eyes and wide cheekbones, he had transformed into an Inca. His voice was darker too, breathless.

'The Oldest Ones can destroy you and take you to themselves that way. When I was small my brother began wasting away. The doctors could not understand it. He was dying for no reason. So my parents took him to a shaman who asked where my brother had been, and they remembered he'd climbed a certain tree. "It is inhabited by the Oldest Ones," he said. "If you cut down this tree he will recover!" And so they did. I was only twelve, but I remember when they cut it down, the tree spilt blood. And after that my brother became well.'

Robert asked: 'Why should the ancestors be so hostile?'

The guide got up abruptly and went and stood outside the tent. The mist had dispersed, to leave a clear night. He called back: 'I don't know why.' He seemed to be struggling with his own ignorance under those threatening stars. 'Perhaps they are envious of the living. They want to draw us back to them.'

JOSIANE'S FEVER never cleared. At night she pitched about in her sleep and uttered inconsequential words, while Louis lay awake, listening. By four o'clock in the morning – 'the evil hour', he called it – he was irked by discordant memories of his own, filled with the stupidity of other people. At this hour he hankered after designing buildings again. When he thought of all the fools concocting hospitals, convention centres and hotels in Hainaut the idea of all that banal industry made his gorge rise. He dreamt of taking a sledgehammer to their pieties in one last, defiant monument. But of course, on an unheroic scale, he had already done so.

He listened to Josiane's breathing in the dark – it had gone quiet – and his moroseness deepened. She had teased him when he told her that a single building had destroyed him. But it was true, and he should have known better. He should have foreseen that the municipal hall of a small provincial town would be assessed by small provincial people. He had not realised how outraged they would be until the day of its inauguration. Standing in a cross-fire of furious incomprehension, on a morning of brilliant sunlight, and flanked by his stony ex-partners – he knew now he'd committed professional suicide – he remembered being suffused by a perverse, peaceful pride. For this was, in the end, his finest creation. And suddenly he forgot those around him – the sad little mayor, the consequential councillors and businessmen, his own peers – and fixed his eyes instead on the thing he had created. He even imagined himself conversing with it. Later he was told that the smile irradiating his face was considered the final arrogance.

The building was ironic and beautiful. Its handsomely carved stone and recessed Ionic pillars – an irreproachably traditional base – supported a façade of sheet glass and steel. But in this functional purity the polygonal windows and concave balconies suddenly challenged pedantic expectations, while above hung a playful skylight of glass and enamelled aluminium.

How they hated it. It gently subverted itself, and they could not understand. It muddled architectural chronology – Greek pillars and sheet glass, good God! – and juxtaposed incompatible materials. What in hell was happening? In the end, of course – and this is what incensed the petit bourgeois – it was saying: everything is contingent, mutable and impure. What a complicated world, my dears! And tomorrow you'll be dead, and the day after no one'll give an *Ave Maria*.

But no, they wanted a world before Auschwitz and Hiroshima. They wanted to be told they were important. That was the building's sin. It was, in its quixotic way, rather classical. It announced: in the scale of things, you are somewhat ridiculous.

# Ten

THRUSTING THROUGH a corridor of cliffs, the river gave the illusion of steering them towards some last mystery. Their mules and horses made no sound over the bridges of tamped earth and brushwood, laid by people who had vanished.

They had left behind the cloud forest now, and were enveloped by an ancient jungle. A hundred and fifty feet above them the trees flowered into a ceiling which dangled lianas and moss and let in no ray of sun. Around them the undergrowth groaned and multiplied in a dreamy tangle of trunks and limbs. Nothing grew clean from the ground, but sprouted from the rotted stumps of its precursors, then put down independent roots into the fermenting earth. Half the trees were intertwined or propped on one another. Often the host trunk had gone altogether, leaving the creepers which had killed it to hang in a dense, self-supporting thicket. Everything was living on the compost of its past, devouring and devoured by it.

Within an hour of sunrise the weariness of yesterday had returned. These mornings they woke up dreading the onset of some insidious sickness, afraid that the dizziness and reeling in their heads would remain. Now they had settled to a slow tramping, less like a party of trekkers than a line of refugees. They listened fearfully to their bodies as they went, conscious of every new pain. By now they were leaning half their weight on the bamboo poles which the guide had cut, trying to lift the stress from the tenderness of their feet. But their arms ached, and the inside of their thumbs grew bloody blisters. Sometimes they looked at one another, Robert thought, wondering who was going to break first.

Whether from rain or dew, the whole forest was wet. Once or twice its canopy parted on the mountains which wedged them in and propelled them unimaginably towards Vilcabamba, and they glimpsed slopes massed with trees which even the guide could not name. Then the jungle closed in again, and they were trudging through twilight. For a long time they heard nothing but faint, continual dripping. Then suddenly an unseen bird would gargle or whoop or let out a lilting grace-note.

Towards noon the guide wondered why the muleteers, who had broken camp behind them, had not caught up. But he could not find any vantage point from which to see back along the path. For a while he slowed his pace. Then, looking sombre and angry, he handed the group over to the cook, and turned back.

The Europeans moved on more slowly. In time, Robert thought, they might all become unhinged. There was an ancient rankness about this forest which was unnerving. The river rushing nearby was no longer mountain-green but brown with the tannin of rotted branches. Emerging eerily beneath their feet were the stones of an Inca road coated in moss and lichens. Once, as they filed beneath a gateway of creepers, they looked up and saw that its piers were made of hewn stone. But whatever it led to had vanished.

Francisco was shivering. The Inca had withdrawn into these shadows to escape his ancestors, and he imagined the conquistadors riding their tough horses down this sombre road, and wondered why they were not afraid. Surely it was like entering the underworld! He glanced down at his blistered hands. Was his blood really theirs?

It was in a narrow clearing that they encountered the men. There were seven of them. They stood across the path without moving or speaking. They simply waited, with their machetes held loosely against their thighs.

Josiane's horse, in the lead, idled to a standstill a yard in front of them, while she remained staring from her saddle, dazed and very pale. Louis's horse crowded behind, then stopped, and the rest of the group fanned out uncertainly. For a moment they remained there, catching their breath and resting on their poles, like skiers unaccountably grounded on an earthen piste. They imagined the men would step aside and shake hands with the weak Quechua greeting. Then their smiles faded. The men did not move.

Louis asked roughly: 'What the hell's going on?'

But the Indians did not resemble any they had seen. They were short and slight. Were it not for their machetes, they might have been children. Their frock-like tunics, reaching to their shins, enhanced the illusion of strange girls. A faint corrugation had gathered between the eyes of several — eyes so far apart that they seemed not to belong together. And the hands which grasped their weapons, like the feet bulging from their sandals, were calloused and black with use.

The smallest man among them – perhaps the oldest – took a step towards them and spoke out. His voice was a guttural stream. It never rose above speaking level, but certain words in it made soft explosions.

None of the Europeans understood.

It was the cook who did. Previously, he had effaced himself, moving always in the guide's shadow. In all these days, none of them remembered him saying anything. But now he conversed in the same aspirated tongue, and his calm was reassuring. Then he turned to the trekkers and spoke haltingly in Spanish. Francisco hovered forward to translate. The Indians' faces stayed unreadable. Everyone waited.

Half dangling from his bamboo poles, Francisco looked like some broken bird, his body inflected courteously towards the Indians, his legs bent by exhaustion.

He said: 'They say we have come to dig up the silver and gold things belonging to those who were before them. That this is their country and we should get out.' He faltered. 'The cook also says they're using a lot of swear words. They say the Inca were their fathers, and that we've come to steal their ornaments.'

'Well, tell them why we're really here!' Louis was red-faced, angry. 'Tell them we're trekkers or campers or whatever the equivalent is.' He urged his horse alongside Josiane's. 'This is idiotic.'

Francisco relayed this back to the cook, who passed it impassively on, while the travellers watched the Indian faces for any reaction. But the Indians looked more than ever like stubborn children, their eyes unfaltering under their matted hair. Their tunics were striped in faded brown and white, like a school uniform, but knotted in place with rope or lianas. Only one had a peaked cap balanced on his head; another wore tattered trousers.

At last the older man replied. His words, by the time they came back, said: 'We know you are going to dig up the things of the dead. When you return this way you must surrender them, so that we can put them back in the ground.'

'They must want the stuff for themselves.' Louis looked as if he were about to spur his horse forward. 'They may be leftover bandits. Are they Sendero Luminoso?'

Robert said to Francisco: 'Tell them we are here to admire their mountains and rivers.' He was watching the stringy hands holding the machetes. 'Tell them we won't be here long.'

The cook spoke this, then backed off. The line of Indians was suddenly breaking up. A cacophony of voices rose from it, the gutturals grown sharp and barking, like the sound of alerted dogs. The older man was being confronted by another, more virulent, and by the man in trousers. The authority was visibly slipping from him. He wore a look of appeasement. The youth in the cap – the biggest, almost fat – loomed in his defence. Perhaps he was his son. But it was impossible to tell the age or status of any of them. Often they appeared merely to be bickering, then suddenly to come close to blows. Their arms still hung at their sides, but their shoulders hunched and lunged in a rancorous language of their own. For a while, almost ritualistically, they seemed to be working something out, defining rank, asserting power, saving honour. But the periods of discord were spinning out of control.

In the uproar Josiane's horse baulked and she nearly fell. Louis dismounted stiffly, angrily, and lifted her down. They stood side by side, her hand wriggled into his. The horses ambled away. Instinctively the whole group was bunching closer, their eyes fixed on the Indians, on the blades gleaming from their fists. Robert moved up behind Camilla and laid his hands on her shoulders. He had meant his grasp to comfort her, but instead it might be transmitting fear. His body was tense and a little numb. Several of the Indians were gesticulating at them. Perhaps Louis was right, he thought: perhaps these were a remnant of the Shining Path guerrillas who had terrorised the region ten years ago. He imagined newsprint, the shock of photographs. Did they line you up beforehand? Or did they make you kneel?

Next moment three of the Indians broke loose. They stepped up against the Europeans and raised their machetes. Josiane gave a scream and crouched against Louis, sinking her head between his thighs. He stooped to hold her, his other hand crushing the fedora on his head, as if to protect himself. Robert and Camilla stood frozen. The man opposite them had lifted himself on tiptoe. The sleeve of his tunic dropped from a sinewy arm. The brandished machete gleamed just behind his head. Robert looked back at him in paralysed conciliation, while the man let out staccato shouts and the blade trembled.

Later Robert wondered about Camilla, whose body was in front of his: wondered what he would have done if the blade had fallen. He did not know. He simply watched as if they were all on film, or in a play. His hands lay leaden on her shoulders, which were utterly still. Meanwhile the Indians went on gesticulating, inciting one another. The hair shook round their faces. Sometimes their voices rose to screams. The Europeans were huddled so close now that they all touched one another. Louis stayed crouched above Josiane, one hand still incongruously on his hat, while Francisco had joined his bamboo poles in front of him with a gesture which looked like prayer.

It was a minute before they realised that the older man and the big youth had joined the others. They were urging something new. Slowly, one by one, the Indians' shouting stopped and their arms dropped to their sides. For an instant there was no sound but fierce breathing.

Then the older man addressed the cook, who was standing alone, and Francisco translated hoarsely: 'He says they will let us go if we return this way. Then they will know we have taken nothing.' He added tensely: 'But he says we must leave somebody behind with them.'

Josiane slithered upright against Louis and opened her eyes. Her face was blotched with fever and she was sweating. He sifted his fingers mechanically through her hair.

The Indians had backed off several paces, murmuring. It was impossible to predict what they would do.

Robert heard his own voice detached from him. 'We can't leave anybody.'

'Then we must go back,' said Louis.

Josiane was only clinging to his shoulder now, releasing him bit by bit. '*Nous allons retourner par le même chemin?*'

'*Mais oui. Un brake doit venir nous chercher à Vitcos. Là, il y a un autre sentier.*'

But Francisco, still leaning like an invalid on his poles, said: 'They think we'll play a trick on them. They say we'll pretend to return, then find another way to Vilcabamba. They demand to have somebody.'

The Indians had retired still farther, and were waiting; but an avenue had opened up among them to receive their prisoner. Robert and Louis looked at one another, and guessed what each was thinking. Louis intermittently laid his hand on Josiane's shoulder, while Robert felt an airy coldness creeping up in him. It was as if a trap were closing. He glanced at the cook, but it seemed to him that the man was no longer on their side. He was gazing hard at the trekkers, as the other Indians were, and he appeared as they did. Even in anger, Robert thought, those faces were unreadable. There was no cruelty in them, and no compassion.

Camilla had followed his glance. Her mouth was tense and her cheeks newly hollow. But she said quite steadily: 'If we leave somebody here, anything can happen to him. He might just disappear.' She turned to Francisco. 'What does the cook think? He must have some idea.'

Francisco asked him, then said: 'He says they are dangerous.'

The coldness in Robert was beating like a great fan under his ribcage. Camilla involuntarily edged closer to him. He turned to stare at the Indians, but nothing had changed. The avenue which waited between their ranks looked like a gauntlet, and they were watching across the sunlit clearing. Only the virulent one had turned away, and was rubbing the flat of his machete across his back, like a sign.

Suddenly Francisco said: 'I'll go.'

He laid down his poles and picked up his rucksack. He saw their faces turned to him. Camilla's especially, the grey eyes radiant in their alarm. For an instant he bathed in them. He imagined he heard her whisper, 'No . . .'

His hands turned and opened at his sides. He thought: *This is what I came for.*

Across the clearing the Indians were stirring a little, sensing a change. In their tunics they might have been resurrected Inca, emerged from the jungle after generations in hiding.

The fear was a part of it, of course. And this tingling submission. And the voices of the others behind him, crying out things. His body pulsating. The few yards across the clearing seemed very long: rumpled earth, some mossy rocks, a dead tree to climb over. Francisco walked across without looking back. Automatically he bowed his head. He did not know if he was trembling with fear or ecstasy. Then the alien faces were around him, and the shining blades. He thought: *This is right, this is what I owe them. This is for Camilla too, and the others, and for all my people's past.*

One of the Indians led him to a tree stump, where he sat down. He saw the cook lingering nearby, and called out: 'Tell them my people have stolen enough from them, and may God bless them.'

The answer came back: 'They say they do not know which your God is.'

He began to feel calmer. One of the men stood guard above him, slanting his machete against his chest. Everything had turned quiet. Francisco eased the hood of his anorak from his bare neck. The sun burnt down on him. His eyes kept returning to the mottled sheen of the machete, and the faint unevenness of its cutting edge.

On the opposite side of the clearing the others appeared

far away. They kept separating then coalescing, looking in his direction. He could pick out Camilla's blue anorak, and her brown head. The cook had gone off to round up the horses. Francisco felt the trembling of his heart subside, but his body still seethed, as if a gentle, continuous charge of electricity were being run through it. He closed his eyes. He thought of those talks in the seminary, about perfect love. Was it possible? And if so, how? And could it last?

Camilla was satisfied, gazing across, that nothing was happening to Francisco. The Indians had simply sat him down. But nobody knew what to do. Josiane was lying on the ground holding her head, Louis touching her from time to time with a helpless roughness on her forearm. 'Ça va? Ça va, toi?' He wanted to leave. But Camilla kept saying: 'We can't go, we can't go.' And Robert said 'Wait for the guide.'

Then Robert walked away into a nightmare realisation of his own.

He went a few yards into the jungle, to be alone. Barely a sunbeam sloped through the trees. He thought: I understand now. Of course. The guide and muleteers are not coming back. They must have known this area was dangerous. They had known it from the start.

The jungle was filled by the noon quiet. It was like a place in ruins. Which way was anywhere? But there was only one track, and some time they would have to take it back. Without the guide, without Francisco.

He turned back to the clearing, where Camilla stood looking across at the Indians. She seemed to stand there in her new separateness, which faintly alarmed him. And he was surprised by her looks: she alone appeared healthier than when they had started out. He wanted to go over to her, but knew she would notice how his hands trembled. She did not yet understand their full predicament, and nor did Louis.

He took out his notebook and forced himself to write. He must remember everything in detail. It was the detail that counted. The way the chins of these people disappeared, and made them moon-faced children. Deceptive. The glitter of the machetes. And the peculiar light in the jungle. The way Francisco walked.

Francisco. How did you write about that? Goodness was never convincing, never interesting. But he wrote: *'Astonishing, the seminarian. Maybe love is simple after all. Irreducible, like a proton. He's no more than a boy: floppy hair over narrow head. Skin an ivory tinge. He walked across like Christ to Calvary. This man and his Christian duty. Shamed us all. The confidence of the conquistadors in his blood.'*

He broke off. The sentences had turned runny and illegible over the page. And he would need this notepad for days now – all his papers were with the mules. He tried to write again, steadying one hand with the other. The clearing was composed like a tableau for his observation, everyone bright-lit and at rest. The Indians stood rather gravely, not talking, their feet planted apart. And Francisco was still sitting with his head bent. The sun pouring down. But after a few minutes Robert stopped. He did not trust his hands to hold a pen. The scene repelled description. If only he could find the defining words, he would understand, and then stop shaking. But he couldn't circumscribe these people, or anything that was happening. The words, the explanations, weren't there, and he felt helpless. Words were a kind of peace. Now they were

117

all at the mercy of these men, whoever they were, and the others did not even realise. When he looked at Camilla, he could not bear it. She had taken off her anorak and was sitting in the sunlight. Her brown arms, brown neck. Waiting for the guide who was gone. He willed the Indians simply to evaporate into the forest; but of course they would not. They wanted more than Francisco. The machetes hung from their fingertips with a suspended purpose. He turned away. Even if he could have formed the briefest note, what was the point? He settled his gaze on the blue circle of sky above the clearing.

THE FIRST muleteer was the tall one, carrying a transistor radio blurting pop music from Lima. Then came the guide in his baseball cap, looking irritated, and behind him the line of men and beasts with their toppling burdens of boxes, tents and canisters. Robert had the impression that the light in the forest had changed, as if a solar eclipse were ending. The poisoned luminescence of the jungle had lifted, and a flood of normal daylight was breaking in.

They waited for the mule-train to reach them. Louis grunted, 'About time!', but bent to grasp Josiane's hand. Camilla was smiling tightly. One of the mules had gone astray, the guide said, and it had taken time to round it up. He stubbed out his cigarette on a rock while he listened to what had happened. Robert, glancing at his watch, saw with astonishment that the guide had been absent scarcely an hour. But who the hell were these people, he demanded, pointing at the Indians, and what did they really want? The tension was pouring out of him.

'They're forest Indians,' the guide said, 'Machiguenga.

They think they guard this jungle. They have some idea that they are the Inca.'

He walked morosely over to them, while the muleteers went matter-of-factly about their business, tightening girths and readjusting loads.

The others watched from a little distance as the Indians gathered to meet the guide. He sounded as if he were haranguing them as they clustered round. The Indian who had been standing like an executioner above Francisco left his post and joined in. Once, they heard the rasping voice of the virulent man, then it quietened, and the guide seemed to be cracking jokes. Even Josiane had clambered to her feet and was watching. She murmured: 'Poor Francisco.'

Louis grunted. There was something disturbing about that young man, he thought. The way he sat there with his head bowed and his wrists crossed, even though nobody had tied them. Louis was reminded of those canvases of – who was it? – Guido Reni or Guercino. All sweet-tinted agony. The Christ figure in his crown of thorns, undergoing a sentimental flagellation. Repellent, seven-teenth-century stuff. And here was this fellow with his simpering eyes and bared neck, posing in the spotlit clearing under this disgusting proscenium of a forest. Worse still, they would all have to be grateful.

The guide was now passing cigarettes among the Indians. They smoked earnestly, self-absorbed, while he continued talking with the older man and the youth. The cook came and went between them and the muleteers, and eventually handed round some biscuits and two old blankets. The Indians began to break up. Francisco had wavered to his feet and was shaking one of the men's hands. Some of them were laughing, even as they disappeared back into the forest.

When the guide returned, with Francisco behind him, he looked contemptuous. 'They just wanted things.' He hitched on his rucksack. 'The Machiguenga are very poor. They were hoping for cigarettes and clothes.'

THAT EVENING, with astonishment, Robert noticed the marks of his fingernails on Camilla's shoulders. They were inscribed there like an indictment.

# Eleven

THEY MADE camp above the river at the village of Vista Allegre; but it was a village only in name. Twelve years ago the Sendero Luminoso had destroyed it, and there was nothing to be seen except a stockaded schoolhouse built of thatch and tree trunks. At sunset three children emerged from the forest to stare at them, and to graze black pigs in the undergrowth. A path behind them reached hidden cottages, where a few farmers had returned.

The cook made supper in the derelict school, where the depleted group of Robert, Camilla and Louis sat among crudely cut benches and tables, and the punctured thatch dropped down insects. Francisco had retired sick to his tent, and Josiane's fever had engulfed her again.

Louis said wretchedly: 'She won't eat. There's nothing left of her.' He was thinking: with this disgusting food, no wonder. And their private rations were giving out. This was not, as he had first thought, one of her periodic malaises, but something more convulsive and alarming.

It was Camilla, in the end, who voiced what they had all been silently wondering. 'You don't think it's malaria?'

The guide shook his head. 'We have no malaria in this region.'

But Louis said: 'Three weeks ago we took a trip in the upper Amazon, to Tambopata. Mosquitoes everywhere. Maybe she got it there.'

'You took the right medicines?'

'Of course we did.'

Robert placed a hand on Louis's arm, and the sympathy from this self-centred man touched the Belgian with apprehension.

'There are many strains that are resistant now,' Robert said. 'And it would have taken two weeks to incubate.'

Camilla said: 'But Francisco's got it too.'

'It will not be the same,' the guide answered. 'He became faint suddenly. I think he has sunstroke.'

They were momentarily silent. They heard the decaying thatch patter onto the tamped earth floor. The candlelight distorted them all, Robert thought, even Camilla, and striated the guide's face with the cheeks and eyes of an Inca.

Louis suddenly said: 'I just want to get her out of here.' Now that the words were spoken, they seemed to create the fact: Josiane had malaria. They must leave. 'How quickly can we get out?'

The guide said: 'We can return to Vitcos in two days and get the jeep from there.'

Louis thrust aside his meal uneaten. For a moment he forgot himself and boomed: 'Can't you call up a helicopter?'

'A *helicopter?*' The guide gave a heartless laugh. 'Look at this country!' After all these days, he thought, the Belgian was still living in a world of e-mail and airports. These spoilt people. How absurd the man's feet looked in their embroidered slippers! He said: 'We're a long day from Vicabamba. There's a village a day's walk beyond that. They might have a telephone. But a four-wheel-drive would get us from there to paved road at Quillabamba in another day.'

'Quillabamba? Is there a hospital?'

'I've never heard of one. In any case, you cannot do much for malaria.'

The guide looked so alien, so cruelly resigned, Camilla sensed he was dreaming of the Oldest Ones, and thinking: the ancestors are devouring her.

'Three more days? Three more?' Louis got up abruptly and barged back to his tent.

The air inside was filled with the fetid smell of the rain forest: the damp that thickened under the groundsheets, filmed every surface, rotted every cloth. Josiane had vomited onto the tarpaulin beside her. She turned hot, frightened eyes to his. He told her the return journey would make no difference either way: forward to Vilca-bamba, or back to Vitcos.

She smiled a watery apology for the mess beside her, for everything gone wrong. '*Je veux arriver à Vilcabamba.*'

CAMILLA WAS woken by a light shining in her face. It was the quarter moon hanging beyond the mosquito net, cupping the wan circumference of its own completion in the sky. She was aware too of a faint noise; but there was no wind, and Robert was breathing evenly beside her. She

*123*

eased from her sleeping-bag, wrapping the cotton dressing-gown round her, listening. It had sounded like a low cry, perhaps an animal.

Outside the tent her bare feet sank in the sward which had once been the village playing field. She stood and listened to the warm night. The tents of the others lay unlit to either side. Mixed with the rustle of the river, she heard the cry again. She kept her eyes on her feet as they crossed the grass, wondering about snakes, and crouched to peer through the mosquito net of Francisco's tent. Now his moans were indistinguishable from those of dreams, but she could hear him thrashing from side to side.

As she stooped under the tent flap, something struck her cheek. It was the enamelled crucifix swinging in the entrance. Francisco lay sprawled under a rumpled sheet in the filtered moonlight. She laid the back of her hand against his forehead. It was burning. His eyes did not open. She rummaged among his things for the flask he always carried, then soaked her handkerchief in its tepid water and touched it to his temples. He stirred as if reminded of something, and looked up. But his eyes seemed dulled. Kneeling above him, she thought he did not realise who she was. He just went on gazing up, a little frightened, while his breathing stilled.

She said: 'Do you want an analgesic, something for your head?' He didn't answer; she added: 'It's Camilla.'

His eyes tried to focus. One of his hands hovered towards her, then curled up on the groundsheet. He said: 'Don't go.'

'I don't know what I can do.'

'Stay.' He eased his body upwards. His shoulders were

*124*

narrow and naked above the sheet, the shoulders of a boy. He said: 'Everything's turning.'

'You have sunstroke.' But she wasn't sure. 'You were too long in the sun.'

'I should not have been there.' His voice was fading, as if he were falling asleep. He murmured: 'Unworthy.'

She said: 'You were far from unworthy.'

But he did not hear. His next words slurred together urgently – they seemed to be about the seminary – and his body started weakly to writhe. She did not know how to treat him, but rested the damp cloth on his forehead and took his head gently in her hands. She was not sure if he could hear or understand, but said: 'We'll stay quiet.'

Yes, he thought in delirium, we'll go out of the moonlight to Our Lady by the seminary in Plasencia. His head was faint, turning. The pain had gone. She floats in blue above the high altar. The cherubs lift her to heaven. Our Lady of Victory, 'She's your favourite, Francisco,' gazes down with slanted eyes. His sickness was returning, the nausea of his helplessness, like some unforgiven sin. If you peer under the cathedral choir stalls at the misericords, they are carved with unspeakable things. Even here.

Camilla looked down at the strange young man with his half-closed eyelids, and from time to time smoothed the dampness from his cheeks. She could not understand anything he said. His head was heavy and his hair flared in a black halo over her lap. He was no longer truly conscious.

She touched his breastbone, and realised that his whole body was on fire, naked under the sheet. She withdrew her hand.

The adoration in his face no longer disconcerted her. In

fact she was conscious of receiving it with a subtly shifted sense of herself. She smoothed back the tangle of her hair. Absurd, she thought, at her age to be reconstituting herself in another's gaze – because what could he possibly be seeing? He seemed less a man to her than a mysterious boy. His tenuous features and nervous mouth were moving below her in their own dream. Then he began to cough, his eyes focused again, and his words separated out: '*Puede ser puro el amor?*'

'What?'

He frowned. 'Love, between people, can it be pure?'

'Pure?' She wasn't sure what he meant. But she said: 'No, Francisco, I don't think so.'

A minute later he drifted back into delirium. He was floating in and out of blackness, beneath Our Lady of Victory, the cruel tenderness of her eyes. When he closed his own he still saw her face. She was beautiful, wasn't she? But he had never touched a woman. He had only ever touched himself, secretly. He noticed the moonlit canvas above her and imagined it a solid ceiling. He mistook the handkerchief for her hand.

The fear came and went. His father was riding above him on his charger; very tall, he commanded infinite land. Yes of course, father, your red-coated cattle, they are the best! Stronger stock! His hair is iron-grey. From beneath his visor you can't read his eyes. But you know they are angry. His horse rears huge, separating him, and streaked with verdigris. '*How have you been wasting your time today?*' Beside the altar St James gallops in full armour. '*In those weeks the Spanish slaughtered six hundred children under three years of age, and burnt and impaled many adults . . .*' Underneath the saint the Inca is pleading, trampled.

126

Father, love me. Father, I too have a birthright. Father, let me love you. Hallowed be thy name.

'It's all right, Francisco.' Her hand feels cold on his forehead.

His head is swimming and seems to have no body attached. Except that his imagined arm is twisted in exquisite pain behind his back. I am the Yellow Inca. Miguel, Miguel, let go of me. You are Pizarro, yes. You are the firstborn. My father loves you. And who is Atahualpa? I am! I am! *'With the Spaniards around him saying a credo for his soul, he was quickly strangled . . .'*

'How can I make reparation?' The words had burst out aloud.

She looks down at him and pours fresh water onto the handkerchief. He is still wandering, she thinks.

'If I am the conquered Inca, I can only make reparation to myself . . . I can only love myself . . .'

She says: 'Yes, yes,' but he does not hear.

In the water under the rock your reflection recognises you. And in the sheen of the machete. They know who you are. 'I love myself.'

'Yes.'

His eyes are closed again. The telephone screams in the Rector's office. Felipe and Carlos, my friends, is love ever pure? With Carlos looking at me like that. All that talk in the Fundamental Moral Theology Class (third year). But even the holy silver is corrupt. Inca blood in the silver chalice of the Host – can it be mingled with His? That silver moves in the processional cross. It encloses the reliquaries of the saints. It crowns the Virgin. *'The right hands were cut off of two hundred Incas in the middle of the square. They were then released . . .'*

127

'Is your arm hurting you?' As he grew quieter she reached down and eased it straight, pulling the sheet from his armpit. Automatically she touched his hair against his face. She saw he had an erection. He was, in his way, beautiful, she thought. His flinching reminded her of her son when Robert was angry. And yes, she wanted to touch him now, to feel his skin against her hands, her breasts.

But she went still. She sensed his life consumed in struggle against the past. She knew this without understanding it. She had always thought that Robert's was the obvious way to be, although she couldn't manage it herself: life as an accumulation of experiences, achievements, enrichings, before you die. But Francisco's was eaten up in sheddings, purifications. There was something she liked about that, a little.

He might be asleep now. She uncushioned his head from her lap and laid it on the pillow of his clothes.

He heard her unzip the mosquito net in the tent flap, and sensed the sudden moonlight against his eyelids. But in a while he forgot that she had gone, and as he drifted into sleep she seemed to continue to sit above him. The censure of her eyes set him at peace.

# Twelve

THEY LOST the next day. Francisco was still weak, and Josiane lay prostrate.

In the playing field which the Sendero Luminoso had turned desolate, they left their tents standing and spent the daylight dozing, waiting and nursing their bodies. The jungle villagers came to the edge of the forest – children with wild eyes and tousled hair, women in their wide Spanish hats – but they never ventured close.

Only Camilla woke at dawn to the whinnying of the horses, and walked for a while along the river, curious at the jungle. Sometimes a single tree harboured a whole gallery of mosses and ferns, and huge *chilka*s grew straight out of the rocks sporting silver berries. She bathed her feet in the river. They looked misshapen. But in England they would soon go back to normal, she thought. Amazing how things did. Above her head the nests of the oropendola birds dangled like string bags from the trees, where they alighted in black and yellow plumage and rippled out peculiar songs. She wondered what Robert was doing.

IN THE shade of the schoolroom he sat with his notes at the luxury of a bare table and stretched his aching leg along a bench. The knee was badly swollen – he wondered if it would need operating on – and a blackened nail had detached itself comically from one big toe.

Nothing worse than yesterday, he told himself, could ever happen to them now. Doggedly he grasped his pad and tried to codify it. Out of the shaking in his mind he wrote: '*Child-like savages. I tried . . .*' But what did he try? Numbness and his body trembling. Try this: '*My wife is under my hands. I can't save her. And I'm meant to be the . . .*' Yet nothing had happened at all. '*The Indians wanted . . .*' But he had never known. Even the guide might have been wrong. '*The Indians wanted . . .*' So my hands tremble. Loss of nerve in middle age. I've become a physical coward. Can I write that?

She was in the doorway, holding a heliconia. 'Look at this one!' But it was just a flower, and already dying. 'I've disturbed you.'

'No. I wasn't doing anything.' He was glad, in fact.

She gazed round at the room. It looked stranger by day. Between the vertical trunks which composed its walls, the outside shone in brilliant green slices. 'I wonder what they learn here.'

'God knows.'

'They're miles from anywhere. Who teaches them? Where do they come from?'

It was mysterious: a school in a jungle where scarcely a soul lived. Yet there was writing on the blackboard. She sat beside him and eased up his trouser leg, then began gently to massage the knee. It was swollen shapeless. His notepad lay open on the table, packed with jagged phrases which she could not read, and black with erasures. For years she had felt a little jealous of these notes: they were like his private code. But when she looked at them now she felt no resentment. His knee was tight under her fingers. Once or twice he winced. He said: 'You're the only fit one left.' He saw her eyes straying over his notebook, and morosely closed it up. 'I'm sure Josiane has tertian malaria. She seems very ill.'

Camilla said: 'And you want her to get worse, don't you?'

He stared at her in surprise. 'What on earth do you mean?'

'That way you can write about it.' She was barely joking. There was a heartless kind of writing men could do (she had noticed this years ago) about somebody who engaged their lust but not their affection.

Robert went on gazing at her. Her grey eyes always moored him to something honest. But he said: 'No, I don't want Josiane to get worse.'

But Camilla's voice held no accusation. She realised with faint shock that she herself cared nothing about Josiane. She said: 'It's not important.' She was taking a tiny revenge on Robert's foolishness. 'I think I understand.'

'You?' He heard himself turning angry. 'How can you understand?'

'I know from my work.' Her certainty surprised her. 'Sometimes in research I find something atrocious, and I'm pleased. I discover that the world's worse than I thought, but still I'm pleased. Because that's my job, to discover things. Then I can say "Look! Look what I've found!"' She added quietly: 'I suppose happiness is boring.'

131

'That's not the same. It's not like hoping someone gets ill.'

She started to laugh. 'But that's a journalist's job, isn't it? Finding material. It would be odd if you didn't care about it.'

'Of course, of course.' He thought: I've done it all my working life. You long for something to happen. The only disaster is nothing happening. Until now.

Already he'd tried to write about Josiane, as if she might find a place in some notional book; he had tried to note the changes in her, and had despised himself not for scrutinising them, but for their shrivelling to fragmentary notes.

*'Curious, she seemed the least vulnerable of us. Because weightless, like an elf. Not heavy enough to come to harm. But now, when fever lifts, very pale and separate. As if not here at all. If she ever was.'*

Camilla had witnessed this over and over again throughout their marriage: his voracity for new experience, however bitter. He was tantalised by any story unravelled and unpossessed. Like a hunter who cannot stop killing.

But now, in a tone she could not identify, he said: 'I don't want anything more to happen.'

'It was hard yesterday.'

He was holding his knee, grimacing, as if to conceal or displace this other pain. 'I mean *anything*.'

She did not understand. He was not looking at her, but down at his bare leg. Then his voice choked: 'Because I can't write it . . . Whatever happens, I can't write it.'

This was what Camilla had been dreading; yet its confirmation came softly – she had already known it,

132

really – and she went on kneading his hot knee, glad to substitute this for the condescension of a caress.

He said: 'I should have offered myself as a hostage like Francisco did.'

She wanted to ask, Why didn't you? But it seemed too cruel. Instead she said: 'I'm glad you didn't.' But it was the kind of thing she had expected of him.

He said simply, not looking at her: 'I was afraid.' He jerked his knee from under her hands – she sensed with astonishment that he felt unworthy of her – and he pulled down his trouser leg. 'I didn't understand what the hell was going on. They might have been kids playing. Or they might have cut off our heads. I just didn't know.'

She tried to tease him: 'You always have to understand!'

'Yes,' then more strongly: 'Yes.' He refused to look at her. 'But instead I just trembled. Didn't you notice? I didn't know what they wanted. What *did* they want? They were just waiting for us to break, weren't they?'

'No, I don't think so. I think they were waiting for us to go.'

'I imagined it was some plot. Between them and the guide, even the cook. I thought they wanted something more.' Even Camilla's steadiness had surprised him. He stood up and turned away from her, facing the blackboard. His gaze wandered over its chalked words: *Rabia es un sustantivo, rabioso es un adjetivo.*

He looked so abject standing there, his shoulders stooped forward, his shirt grey with sweat, that she wanted to hold him. So he had found no words by which to understand his own humiliation. He could not pretend in writing – or in anything else, she thought (she had always loved that in him). So he had gone dumb.

But she held back from touching him. His own pride deflected her, of course. But a sense of preservation had also surfaced, a refusal to drown with him. She recognised this as a precious new solitude. She did not want to relinquish it. So she went on gazing at his back, half tenderly, half in surprise at this alienation: that she could look at him as if he were somebody else, even as she imagined her past self clasping him.

In the end she said: 'How could any of us have known anything?'

He answered: 'I just want this journey to be over. I'm starting to hate this whole country.'

She murmured: 'It's beautiful.'

But he didn't hear. 'I'll see what to do when we get home.' He was growing unrecognisable to himself. In a minute, he thought, everything was going to repel him: not just himself, but this land, these people, even Camilla.

THAT AFTERNOON Robert passed Francisco's tent, then turned back on an impulse and stooped through its flap. He was no longer irritated by the way Francisco stared at Camilla. He even relished her a little in his eyes. Now the man was lying on a bare groundsheet, gazing at the tent ceiling, and took a second to focus on him. Then a faint smile crossed his face.

Absurd, Robert thought, how hard it was to utter, but he said: 'I want to thank you for what you did yesterday, Francisco.' He added quietly: 'You're a good man.'

The smile vanished from Francisco's face. Robert was astonished to see him grimace with pain. He said: 'No, I'm not a good man.' Then his own words appeared to ignite something in him. He said more loudly: 'How can you think that?' Suddenly he was shouting with a hoarse anger, so that the whole camp must have heard, and the forest beyond: 'I'm not a good man! No! No! I'm not a good man!'

# Thirteen

THE JUNGLE which enveloped them on the last miles to Vilcabamba was sunk in deeper stillness than before. For miles they might have been climbing and descending along the floor of a green ocean. The only sound came from invisible troops of howler monkeys – not howling at all, but making an unearthly, muffled roar, like gathering thunder. Then suddenly the track would loose them along a precipitous valley-side where they glimpsed the river frothing below, and the slopes opposite curtained in cyclops trees and the surge of bamboo.

Once or twice they passed farms where maize grew, or coffee, or passionfruit trees. But they never saw who worked them. Then the jungle closed in again. The rocks underfoot were slithery with recent rain, and the earth stuck like clay. They were too tired to speak. At last Camilla found herself longing to ride, but even the mules looked jaded, and she did not ask. The jungle passed her by in a daze of new orchids and birds: trogons and oropendolas and handsome blue and black tanagers.

She felt irritated by Josiane, even now. In the girl's

subtle way, this was probably where she always managed to be: the object of everyone's concern. But Josiane rode in front with an inanimate stiffness, and her hands had dropped from the reins. She never ducked the leaves and vines which swept her face. She looked only straight ahead. Louis stumbled alongside, often with his arm lifted to her waist. She did not seem to notice him. One of the muleteers – the tall one, still cradling his transistor radio – was leading her horse by its bridle.

Once Robert came alongside and laid his hand on Louis's shoulder. 'Should we be doing this? Do you want to stop?'

'No. I want to get her to a hospital.' Robert was shocked by the change in him. The flesh of Louis's face had sagged, leaving his eyes bulging out of ash-grey circles. 'She wants to get to Vilcabamba.'

Robert looked up at her and found no recognition. She was clasping her head now. He wondered what she imagined Vilcabamba to be. He said: 'The guide thinks we'll reach there by sunset.'

Louis just said: 'We'd better.' He was concentrating on holding her. Sometimes they pushed through gullies so narrow that the rock scraped her knees on either side, and he had to fall back and leave her balanced in front of him. He was condemning himself again that any of this had happened. Yet it had come so fast. Barely had they sidestepped civilisation than they fell into this morass. They were right to hate the jungle, he thought. It carried no form, no memory. It just surrounded them with this poisoned timelessness. Trees like wrecked umbrellas. The whole forest moist, dripping. And everywhere these insect-riddled leaves, and moss-smeared rocks like green turds. The only other colour was the blood-red bells of datura shrubs, the tone of tarts' lipstick.

They passed dead snakes and revolting, iron-coloured slugs which exuded poisonous milk when trodden on. Everything strong in this forest was clasped about by others – lichens, bromeliads, lianas – until it toppled to the earth in a blurred column of parasitic green. Nothing was distinguishable from anything else: everything eating or devoured in an ancestral cannibalism.

Only towards late afternoon did Louis become conscious of a new strangeness. His arms had long ago ached from supporting her, and had dropped to his sides, so that he watched her moving ahead of him still upright in her saddle, held there by some long-learnt equilibrium. Gradually he acknowledged that around her head – and exclusive to her – fluttered a cloud of butterflies: blue and black, orange and blue. He despised himself for this sentimentality, yet his gaze kept returning to them. They accompanied her like a benediction.

NONE OF this was clear to Robert, who was falling behind. Every time he jarred his foot, his knee shot up pain. He began counting the steps. The only person in sight was Camilla, who had lagged behind on purpose. He watched her from time to time with suppressed confusion. She looked crisper against the jungle, more isolated. A child, he fancied, might have cut her out and stuck her in a scrapbook, as something separate. Twice he tried to catch her up, but never succeeded, and he realised she was matching her pace to his, trying to encourage him. This tactfulness at once touched and annoyed him.

Only once, where a tributary formed a pool, did the

guide stop to let him catch up. The pool's edge was lined with fresh-cut flowers; it was one of those signs that there were other people here, others they never saw.

The guide said: 'They leave flowers to keep peace with the *sirena* in the water. So she makes good reflections of them.'

He set off remorselessly down the track.

But the guide was longing to get back to Cuzco. There were people, even foreigners, who fitted this land, he thought. You felt easy with them. But this party looked like a file of ghosts. The Spaniard gave off something troubling: he appeared ill beyond sunstroke, and could scarcely take his eyes from the Englishwoman. Perhaps he was a little mad. Two of the mules had gone lame, and the journalist was limping badly. But worst of all was the French woman. He was sure she had cerebral malaria. She kept holding her head. He could smell that she was no longer continent, and now her sweat was attracting butterflies.

Towards evening they emerged on a spur overlooking the valley of Vilcabamba. The jungle flowed down and powdered it in mist, and beyond it the sealing mountains were touched with broken sunlight. It looked a place of enclosed peace. A natural end. The guide said: 'That's Espiritu Pampa, the Plain of Spirits. The river goes by Vilcabamba.' He pointed. 'There.'

They followed his arm, but as usual they could descry nothing. They went on gazing down without a word, leaning on their poles like walking wounded. It was hard to tell if Josiane or Francisco were seeing anything at all. Only Louis burst out: 'Thank God for that!'

A CLOUDLESS dawn broke over their camp. They had bivouacked in darkness, and Camilla and Robert woke to see that farmers had cleared oases in the jungle – a banana grove here, a potato field there – and that their tents stood in pasture.

A narrow path led towards Vilcabamba, and they ventured halfway down it. The forest heaviness had lifted. The air was cool, and a young sunlight fanned across the treetops. They walked very quietly, Camilla afraid to waken the jungle, Robert willing it to show them something. For the first time, they realised, they were led by no one – no guide, no horse, no mule – but quite alone.

They went as if on tiptoe. They imagined they left no trace in the silence. Then they came to a place where the tree canopy lifted very high. It glittered two hundred feet up in a translucent sky of sun-polished leaves. And across this heaven an animal was moving. It crept with unearthly slowness, oblivious of them. It was an arboreal anteater. They stopped dead, staring up, while it cruised in archaic profile across the filtered sun. It seemed to be sleepwalking out of another age, repudiating theirs. Involuntarily their hands reached out and clasped one another. And the creature stole away across their skyline and into the shadow.

ALL MORNING and into the afternoon nobody went to the ruins. They all seemed to be waiting for Josiane. But a nervousness had settled over them, a reluctance to confront the site in case – after a hundred and fifty miles of this ordeal – they were to find nothing much at all. Josiane was suffering convulsions, Louis said; she was barely

141

conscious. He was racked with apprehension. So they waited in their tents or wandered along the jungle's edge, feeling a muted alarm. Even here, just half a mile away, Vilcabamba seemed less a place than a region in their minds.

In the afternoon a few farmers came and sat among the muleteers, conversing in murmurs, and the news of trouble must have spread, because later others appeared holding shy gifts: a handful of papayas or a piece of chicken. The courtesy in these offerings – tendered by men in old anoraks and sandals, women in tattered skirts – seemed to rise out of an ancient civilisation. They filled Francisco with shame. He lay exhausted on the grass, afraid to go to the ruined city, and watched the Indians returning to their thatched huts where they slept on beaten earth.

Later he heard heavy feet over the grass. Then the Belgian loomed explosively above him. His denim suit sagged discoloured around his coarse body, and was torn at the collar. He was even more alarming like this. He was seething with frustration. He said: 'My wife wants you to say Mass for her.'

Francisco groped to his feet. He could not imagine saying Mass for anyone, let alone Josiane. He shook his head.

Louis boomed: 'Why not, man? What's wrong with you?'

'I can't. I'm not a priest.'

Louis looked as if he might hit him. 'You're a deacon, aren't you? Well then? Well then?'

'I'm not even a seminarian. I left . . .' I'm unworthy, he thought. Don't you see? I'm less than you are.

'But you can still give the Sacraments!' The Belgian's hand tipped an imagined cup in the air. Even as he enforced his wife's request, he seemed to despise it. Francisco had the impression that he tossed the aerial cup over his shoulder.

Then Louis asked quietly: 'Can you confess her?'

Francisco imagined trying to catch the whisper from that porcelain mouth. He could not conceive anything it might say. She repelled him for no reason he understood. But he thought: what I feel for her is unimportant – I am just a means, a vehicle.

He said: 'It's true I may give the Sacraments' – even if the channel of grace was depraved, it could carry incorruptible the blood of Christ – 'but no, I can't confess her.'

'Can't you even listen to her? She's suffered! She needs to speak! She suffered as a child. She's half delirious. Can't you listen?'

Francisco thought: how suffered? To him Josiane looked unscathed, as if nothing had ever been inflicted on her. She was a creature of urban artifice. Surely any pain would have shattered her to bits. He said: 'I can't absolve her. I have no authority.'

'Well just give her the Sacraments then! Give her anything. Comfort her, comfort her!' Louis pulled a half bottle of wine from his hip pocket and thrust it at Francisco. 'Give it to her. Do whatever you do.'

So Francisco followed him to their tent, and crawled inside alone. He felt afraid of what he might find there. He thought: I do not know who she is. I have never known.

She lay in her sleeping bag with a blanket loose at her neck, although the air was warm. Her face was drained, its make-up gone. Her chin tilted at the ceiling. She looked like the tourist girls he'd seen in Trujillo. Ordinary. A line of down showed on her upper lip. Louis's voice, or even God's, resonated in his head: comfort her.

To his own astonishment he found a plate and chopped at a stick of bread, then poured a little wine into a coffee cup. But he knew he had no power to consecrate them: so what could they be? Just a baguette and some claret. He dipped the one into the other. Perhaps he was in mortal sin. Her eyes stayed closed while he turned and knelt by her head.

He felt a curious peace. In his undeservingness he had perhaps been blind to her. His own corruption had blinded him. She lay very still while he pressed the bread inside her lips. 'The Body of Christ . . .' So she was not evil at all. Only he was evil. She looked like a stricken child. Her hands emerged from the blanket and steadied his. The silk nightdress reached to her wrists. Her fingernails were all broken. He thought suddenly: God is preparing her for death. Some crumbs of His spurious Body dribbled down her chin and neck, and he dabbed them away. The sin is mine, he thought, only mine. Her violet eyes opened. She faintly smiled. He could hear only the beat of his own heart.

Suddenly she began in a small, hoarse voice: 'When I was eight . . . I was only eight . . .'

He said quickly, softly: 'I can't hear confession.'

'. . . my father . . .'

'I'm just a deacon. I can't absolve you.' He put down the coffee cup, empty. He imagined her saying unspeakable things.

But she had closed her eyes again, and seemed to be

144

drifting into unconsciousness. He traced the sign of the cross over her head.

# Fourteen

S HE WAS supposed to be the caring one, of course, the only other woman in the party, so it was natural she should play nurse to Josiane. As she gathered her futile aspirin and vitamin tablets into a washbag with a last bottle of mineral water, she felt a wary irritation, threatened by emotions she did not want to feel. Josiane was young, she told herself, and would recover.

But as Camilla crouched into Josiane's tent she was horrified by the change in her. Her face had shrunk to a scaffold of small bones like those of some rodent, and a web of burning veins crept and bulged about her closed eyes. And Camilla saw with misgiving that the flush along her cheeks — once indistinguishable from rouge — had deepened to a purplish inferno which looked as if it would never fade.

She was afraid at once that there was nothing she could do, but she busied herself with the mineral water, touching its spout to Josiane's lips — which did not drink — and pressed a wet flannel to her forehead. But whereas Francisco's temples had sweated out of a soft, breathing skin, Josiane's flesh felt shiny and impermeable, resistant to her touch. She was reminded, with a shudder, of the mummy at Vitcos. Again she tried to inveigle the bottle between Josiane's teeth; then she realised they had clenched with pain. The girl was convulsed by some mute inner agony. Camilla went on passing the cloth over her forehead like a prayer. The perspiration leaked from it in grit-like beads, but Camilla felt she might as well have bathed a stone.

She feared that if Josiane slipped altogether into unconsciousness she would not come back. So she spoke against her ear: 'It'll be all right . . . It's Camilla here . . . It'll be all right . . . Josiane . . .'

For a long time she thought she went unheard. The words merely comforted herself with an illusion of conversation. Josiane made an odd, metallic breathing.

'Josiane, we're all here . . . Louis is here . . . This is Camilla . . .'

The girl's eyes opened and looked at her. Camilla had never before felt these eyes to be quite real, more like decoration. But now they were burning lavender. They fixed her with a fevered penetration, as if there was something urgent she wanted to say or know. She made tiny mewings though her clenched teeth: *'Me sens pas bien . . . mais pas du tout . . .'*

Camilla said: 'It must pass. It will pass.'

*'Quand?'*

'Soon. It will.' She touched her hand to Josiane's head. The drenched cowlicks circled it like discoloured claws. 'Is there anything you want?'

Josiane did not seem to hear. She said in English: 'I'm sorry.'

Camilla bent closer. 'Sorry for what?'

But she whispered: 'What is Vilcabamba like?'

'We haven't been.' She added: 'We're waiting for you.' She realised this was true.

The girl said: 'I hold you all back.'

Of course she did, Camilla thought; but nobody had said it until now. Hotel reservations, air flights: she'd forgotten they existed.

Josiane said again: 'I'm sorry.' Then her eyes shut and her face contorted into its torture, and she was no longer seeing or hearing anything except the furnace inside her skull.

Camilla leant across and held her shoulders. Their bones moved fleshless under her hands. She wanted to lift her a little, but Josiane's head sagged onto the pillow of clothes. It was the sight of her neck – its eggshell skin, its stem-like thinness – that made Camilla afraid. She eased her back and settled helplessly beside her. After a minute she felt tears trickling down her own face. She dashed them away. She was crying: 'Damn . . . Damn . . .' But they erupted again when she thought they had stopped.

For a few minutes Josiane endured the pain until the spasm eased. Then she opened her eyes again. 'Can I see myself?'

Camilla delved into her washbag and placed its mirror between Josiane's fingers.

The girl lifted it towards her face, then dropped it and cried out like a child: 'I want *my* mirror!' She scrabbled hysterically for her handbag, and held the glass against her face.

Camilla felt her old disgust. She stayed quiet, cold,

while Josiane sought herself out in the glass. She wondered: what will she see staring back at her?

Josiane frowned and dropped the mirror onto her blanket with a little 'Oh.' It was an abrupt sound, more bewildered than surprised, and now she lay still.

Perhaps, Camilla thought, she had simply wanted to confirm her existence beyond the fire in her head.

'You'll soon look better.'

Josiane shut her eyes. She whispered: '*Ça n'a pas d'importance.*'

Camilla sensed her sinking back into delirium. Her body started to tense and arch in the sleeping-bag. Once her hands came up and clutched her head. Camilla imagined she could see their bones quivering, and the pulsing in the veins which latticed half her face. From time to time Josiane would surface and utter disconnected words. And it seemed to Camilla that the dream she was living as she tossed and muttered was her only coherent life now, and that consciousness was too painful to hold it. So she did not interrupt, only went on touching her cloth to the clenched face, and felt a hollow ache in her stomach. Josiane is younger than me, she thought, and I believe she is going to die.

Then: '*Est-ce qu'un mal pourrait faire craquer la tête?*' The girl's eyes were half open. 'Madame Rivoire said that . . . your head can fall off with pain . . .' She let out a ghost of her irritating laugh. But now it sounded precariously brave.

Yet Camilla was unsure if Josiane was conscious of her presence any more. She thought she might go back to Robert, who was trying to cheer up Louis in the dining-tent. She even murmured this.

But Josiane asked suddenly: 'Does Robert like Louis?'

Camilla answered in surprise: 'Yes, I think so.'

She went silent again. Camilla could not tell what she was feeling. Outside in the dusk a jungle bird or animal was screaming, but in notes repeated again and again, like a song. Then Josiane said: 'Do you think they stop us living . . .'

Camilla only guessed what she meant. She could not tell if the glitter in the girl's eyes rose from urgency or fever. But she said: 'If we let them.' It seemed important to get everything right now. 'What do you think?'

'I think so.' Josiane's voice was almost gone. 'I thought Louis . . . then . . .'

This strange intimacy was the closest Camilla heard. Later she thought about it, what it meant; and because these were Josiane's last words to her, they lingered like a wound.

But Josiane was returning to delirium. Her hands lay open beside Camilla's: hot, thin fingers with split nails. Camilla took them in hers, and they clasped her weakly back. This frail pressure rent her heart: not simply for Josiane – she did not know Josiane – but for some woman mislaid in that wrecked and childless frame. She even had the nostalgic fancy that the female in herself was dying in Josiane – all that self-care and passive tenderness slipping away, and youth perhaps – as the girl sank towards coma.

NEXT MORNING Louis felt reassured. His wife had passed a quieter night, and he thought her sleep was the sleep of exhaustion. Her breathing came softer and more regular. Outside their tent the air felt moist and the valley was filling with clouds. The muleteers were busy binding the

*151*

foreleg of one of their beasts, and a few farmers had gathered on the edge of the pasture to watch. These people made Louis uneasy – they seemed to be waiting for something – and he blatantly outstared those who came close, until they retired. Later in the morning one of their women – a meddlesome pigmy in an incongruous Spanish hat – came cringing into his tent with a piece of boiled *cinchona* bark for Josiane. It looked like a dirty sock. He kicked her out.

But towards noon he became anxious. Josiane had not stirred. When he tried to wake and feed her she wouldn't even sip water. Once she raised her arms and held his head as if to comfort him. Then she went back into sleep. And by the evening he had grown alarmed.

JOSIANE WAS adrift in an ocean of ebbing pain. The diseased cells were massing along the capillaries of her brain, and shutting it down. She dreamt she was on the way to Vilcabamba with a group of others whom she did not know. They were riding under an empty sky. The man beside her was her father, who had been dead for seventeen years. They passed some fashion houses and a riding school. There were a few people about, people she did not recognise, and some dogs. The jungle lapped the city on three sides, and they approached it along a causeway over a lake. By now it was night, and the water filled with stars.

As the infected cells coagulated and cut off the lifeline to her mind, Louis lay beside her in exhausted sleep, and sensed nothing. Through the open tent flap the Inca stars glittered, and shone in the lake of Vilcabamba. Her horse's hooves drifted without sound over the causeway. They had little farther to go.

# Fifteen

HE WAS wounded in some inaccessible part of him. He knew this mainly by the way he walked: in short, trembling steps, as if he had suffered a stroke. He went a short way up the track towards the ruins, skirting mud and puddles, then sat down facing an orchard where black and white pigs rootled. Louis wanted to gaze on nothing. His body was light to him, unnecessary. This was as far as he would go to Vilcabamba. He wanted never to see it.

He had grown old overnight. The weariness which had always threatened him – a malaise lurking beneath the grossest pleasures – had now risen and engulfed him. He recognised it not as some grief which time would ease, but as the intrinsic fabric of his being, from which Josiane had shielded him.

Now that the muleteers had taken her away, to be carried ahead of them in a foetal bundle, lashed to her horse – bodies rot fast in this climate, the guide said – he had nothing left to do or think. Within a few hours the future had withered. He knew he would leak away into it, drop by drop. He had no desires left. There was nothing now between himself and dying. Except his rage against life itself, its savage idiocies. Already he was starting to roar inside, and this would intensify, he knew. It would become a bitter, unfocused rancour which would last him through to death.

From all this she had saved him. By her child's beauty, by her need of him, by her naive cleverness (which she denied), she had salvaged him from pointlessness. He had imagined himself growing old, nursed by her, unafraid that she would have affairs (she did not need them, he understood this). He had lamented only the prospect of her widowhood in middle age. Instead . . . He thought: I have been indulging a dream. I loved the odour of sanctity about her, of childishness. It was like a redemption, at my age. The next moment he was feeling: my survival is absurd. I'm like a snail shell left behind. But I can never afford to be still again.

All afternoon the others came into his tent with that respect for mourning which subtly alienated them. They did their best. He felt sorry for them. But they made him feel diseased. Only the guide seemed comfortable and practical with death, and the soft handshakes of the muleteers – they lined up outside his tent – appeared to transmit a physical sympathy.

Their little group, he realised, had coalesced in fear. The English couple did not know whether to abandon or to smother him. How could he tell them that he resented their health? Why were they alive and not she? When Camilla hugged him, he felt her solidity, her fullness, as if she were another species from Josiane, with no echo of that delicacy in her body. Her embrace left only another loneliness. How did you deal with death? It had no meaning. It overlooked the ugly and the stupid. It left behind himself. And took her. Good God, why couldn't it have taken the sour journalist or the narcissist priest?

Camilla said haltingly: 'Josiane . . . she was so sweet . . .'

Sweet. Louis guessed she hadn't liked her. He didn't care. Josiane was his, not theirs. In any case, you never knew what the English were feeling: this veiled, self-complicated people.

Only with Robert – was it a moment of weakness? – he asked: 'This book of yours?'

The Englishman shrugged his shoulders. He looked wretched. But of course, Louis thought, he had to pretend grief.

Louis said: 'If you write it, put her in. A small sketch of her. She wanted that. Just the way she rode her horse or the look of her face.' Christ, he thought, have I become an imbecile? The man will write something mawkish. But it was true, she had wanted it. And Louis – if he was honest, yes – to him too it might be a token to outlive decay, a memorial of sorts. Even if it did not portray the woman he had known, even if it were false (and who could be sure?), it would register the trace of her.

Robert looked abashed, and Louis imagined he guessed what he was thinking. 'Yes, I know. I laughed at your ambitions to write, I did! But I meant no offence, Robert. Myself, I can't write a sentence without sweating.'

Robert began: 'I'll try, of course I'll try. At present it's hard . . .'

Louis burst out: 'Well, forget it if you can't!' For a moment he remembered his old self. 'It's probably all bogus, trying to recreate somebody in words. Remember the Inca!' He thought: yes, their *quipu* was the only true literature – a hard tally of facts and figures. They must have rejected the alphabet on purpose.

Perhaps they were afraid that writing would replace memory.

'WE SHOULD *have known she was going to die . . . She sat her horse with an odd, fey transience. Her eyes . . .*'

This is idiot stuff, Robert thought. Damn you, Josiane, what did you mean to me? Already I find it hard to recall how long or short your nose was, and it takes several seconds to rediscover the precise timbre of your voice. I'm writing as if I loved you. (He crumpled up the paper.) But I'm only mourning something which never happened. Just nostalgia for the imagined. I remember a young woman photographing lilies.

Yesterday he had entered her tent to offer what help he could, and had seen her head tilted in photogenic profile on the pillow, just as she had described the face of one of her dead patients. Was she dying herself then, or already gone? He didn't know. She hadn't moved. And he? At first he felt only a kind of frozen pity. Then he thought: how odd she looks. How the thread-like veins have darkened over her closed eyelids. And somewhere in the back of his mind the thought lodged itself: I can use that.

Yes, that is what she meant to me, he thought: a dark-veined eyelid.

A LITTLE furtively, hoping to avoid the muleteers as they trussed the body onto a horse, Robert and Camilla took the overgrown path to the ruins. Neither of them wanted to pass her cortege as it moved on towards the distant police post at Quillabamba, or listen to the men's shouts, or to the half-broken transistor. They followed where an Inca road had once descended towards the city, its stones vanished under the loose earth.

Robert could not keep the irony from his voice. 'So Louis asks me to write about her.'

'He hopes you'll do what she wanted.'

Robert kept his eyes on his feet. They stepped between tree roots squirming from the soil. 'Well, I can't. I can't.'

'If you can't imagine completing a book' – her words came carefully – 'you could write a piece on her and send it to Louis.'

Robert said: 'I can't do her justice.' He stopped in the shadows of the avenue, and turned to face Camilla, but stared beyond her shoulder. 'It's better to shut up.'

That was why he could not describe this journey, or evoke the Inca. Didn't she see? The talent wasn't there in him; he had only thought it was. He began in a hoarse, self-lacerating voice: 'You know I've always imagined I was a hack journalist from necessity. But in fact it's quite natural to me!' His laugh erupted as a cough. 'I assumed there was something more powerful in me, of course. I thought all I had to do was give it a chance.'

But he had opened the floodgates, and a little sand had trickled out.

He added: 'How can I write about Josiane? I don't feel right about her. I don't even know what Louis is expecting.'

'He's expecting a simple paragraph! Can't you even do that?' She was suddenly angry. It happened so rarely, it chilled him. 'You're trying for too much, Robert, that's your trouble. Why should you be feeling anything important?' She was standing with her hands tucked casually into her anorak pockets, but her eyes were blazing. 'Just do something modest!'

She ached to tear him down, plant him in solid earth. He always felt that things went deeper than they did. And he imagined there was more in everyone than there could be (she had suffered from this). He would not accept that life was often little, or that death could be meaningless.

His voice trembled slightly. 'I didn't understand her.'

'There may not have been all that much to understand.'

He wondered for a moment if Camilla was jealous, then thought no: she is just telling me something.

She said more calmly: 'You're trying to stir up some significance because she's dead. Whenever you don't understand something you elevate it into a mystery.'

But her voice was quietening half into affection. She understood how he feared evanescence, had feared it since his parents' dying. And if death was anything, it was time passing.

He could not find anything to say, and they started to push on faster down the meandering path. The jungle was speckled with sunlight, and a few dishevelled steps had emerged underfoot.

After a long time he said: 'When I last saw Josiane she'd lost consciousness. I didn't know what to do, so I just stayed beside her. Then I noticed the mauve veins over her eyelids. I consciously noted them in case I should need . . .' He glanced at her. 'You would never do that.'

No, he thought, Camilla was another creature altogether. He imagined her as an earlier and more healthy form of life, from which he was a mutant. Her realness was even a little mysterious to him, and he imagined he could attain it only by a complicated shedding of himself. In fact he might spend all his life reaching the state to which she had naturally been born.

'Well, I'm not a writer,' she said. 'I have a poor imagination.'

'But you feel appropriate things. You feel properly.' That was why he loved her.

'Not always,' she said.

'I think you despised Josiane, but after you last saw her you came back wretched.'

'I felt sorry for her. She seemed unfulfilled.' Camilla remembered what Josiane had said about men. 'And she was in pain.' No, she thought, I do not feel appropriate things. In Josiane I even felt my girlhood dying, as if she were taking away some part of myself. Even the capacity to love.

She could not say this to Robert – at least not now – but Josiane's unlived life had startled an echo in her own – a fleeting and distorted sound which she had not yet absorbed.

Robert said: 'I sometimes felt she wasn't really there.' His knee cartilage was starting to throb again. It occurred to him that this pain might have blurred and disfigured everything.

'Don't idealise her.' Camilla's plea sounded for him, not for herself. 'Don't destroy her memory. Just write something simple. That's all Louis wants: a girl on a horse.'

He said: 'I'll try.'

The sun had slanted from sight, shifting the leaf-patterns of the jungle out of their path. They were both wondering if the muleteers had finished their task, and how soon it would be before they were on the move again. A few birds began crying in the forest. It occurred to them both that in the cold light of England all this would fade away like a nightmare, and that everything might return to how it had been. But they were not sure.

Soon even the refracted sunlight of the treetops had gone, and silence filled the jungle. They crossed a stream by an Inca bridge so sunk in soil they barely noticed it, and found themselves in an artificial clearing. Everywhere its earth heaved and dipped with unnatural shapes, so that Robert had the idea that all Vilcabamba lay underground like an abandoned cemetery. Their feet fell soundless over the powdered soil. They were quite alone. Here and there enormous silk-cotton trees pushed their roots like white snakes through piles of stones.

Then they realised that they were walking through a whole city. It broke surface in a blurred geometry of terraces and streets. But everything that had once been clear and defined was split by creepers, which had rattled loose its stones and left a detritus of fallen twigs underfoot.

Camilla left Robert to wander alone, while she sat with her back to a rock and listened to the cicadas. Her legs and arms were throbbing gently, her whole body tingling as if in delayed resurgence.

But Vilcabamba would never resurrect itself in the glistening surge of palaces which Robert had once playfully imagined. Instead he was walking where its bones had faded into the earth. They showed no trace of strength or richness. The mossed ruins seemed half returned to vegetable matter. Here and there a doorway had been cut smooth, or a niche or fountain spout dimpled a drystone wall. But that was all. The whole city had sunk beneath the overwhelming weight of the forest.

Yet its forms and purposes were all recognisable to him,

like an old ache: ceremonial platforms and plazas, dormi-
tories, temples and a huge, worshipped stone. He even had
the feeling that his weakness prevented him from seeing
them truly, that these familiar shapes – which two weeks
ago had fascinated him at Choquequirau – still gleamed
pure here in the jungle, and that it was only he who had
faded.

His whole leg was on fire now, so that he used his sticks
as crutches. But his head felt cool and faint. Where was
Vilcabamba? Was it really this? No script commemorated
it. It would have survived in oral memory, but there was
nobody left who remembered.

In this trance, he left his notepad behind under a kaypoc
tree, and forgot to go back and search for it.

Instead he wandered without motive, recreating nothing in his head – no history, no order – as if dreaming.
Here and there some peasants had cleared the undergrowth from the ruins and exposed them in lines of loose
masonry. But already the jungle had seeded itself in the
mortarless cracks, and was swarming back over the walls.
Its silence was ruffled only by the grating of the cicadas
and the trickle of an invisible stream. He went on
wandering in hypnosis at the bright collage of leaves and
stones, the slow sinking of steps and doorways into the
powdery earth, where the Inca had retreated into their
illiterate silence.

THAT NIGHT they made love for the first time in weeks.
Under their tent's dome, lit by the stars, Robert reached
out to her with the uncomplicated need of a child. In his
arms he felt her body flowing out to him, very strong and

full, as if she were physically replenishing him, and he cried out her name.

Yet he realised he had not repossessed her. Rather he sensed the arousal of her pity – her fingers threaded his hair – and then felt this pity turn sensual, so that she embraced him as she might have cradled their son, with a half-erotic tenderness. Even in his exhaustion, this imbalance touched him with a muffled warning, and when his lips travelled along her neck, her shoulders, even her mouth, they seemed to be paying court to something tender, but subtly inviolate.

# Sixteen

THE SUN rose cold above the forest. The dawn rustlings and murmurings of the undergrowth faded, and the silence of daylight came down. Walking among the ruins of Vilcabamba, his footsteps crackling like gunshot over the twigs, Francisco tried to make sense of the walls worming out of the earth. Even to his unpractised eye, these buildings had been raised without wealth or time. The city had lasted barely thirty years before his people wrecked it. The few details left – a lintel here, a niche there – looked grimly makeshift.

As he trudged over its terraces, this sadness grew like a malaise. In its poverty, the place seemed defenceless. The doggedness of its builders struck him with bitter pathos. They seemed to be saying: let us be. These are our familiar shapes and structures. They have no power left, but they are ours. Leave us.

But the Spaniards did not leave them. They had burnt the sacred mummies and carried off the golden idol of the sun into obscurity.

And what was he doing here? Perhaps after all, he

thought, my ancestors are doing penance in me. That is why pain is sweet. Yet he felt estranged even from his own body. The softness of the heaped earth silenced everything, covered the city with a grey carapace. He felt lighter than its dust. The stones and foliage shimmered and coalesced over the dry ground. He glanced down in alienation at his feet in their frayed trainers. Several times he imagined they overtrod the print of armoured boots, but left no mark of their own. And how odd these hands were, furled over their sticks! Blistered and scabbed, they looked like someone else's.

Here and there, where a chamber was still intact, he imagined that the Inca themselves had shrivelled: the doorways looked unnaturally low. And although he knew this was caused by the debris risen beneath them, he could not dispel the idea that his people's victims had been physically reduced.

Yet the Inca had imagined Vilcabamba a paradise, and had recreated here the sacred landscape of their lost homeland: worshipped rocks and mountains. Francisco gazed across at such a rock – huge and once holy – rearing from the twilit jungle. The walls around it had been sucked back indecipherably into the ground. As if to spike his conscience, he whispered aloud the description he had read in books. *'The climate is such that bees make honeycombs like those of Spain in the boards of the houses, and the maize is harvested three times a year. In it are raised parrots, hens, ducks, local rabbits, turkeys, pheasants, curassows, macaws, and a thousand other species of birds of different vivid colours. The Incas had a palace on different levels, roofed with tiles, and covered entirely with a great variety of paintings in their style. The doors of the palace were of very fragrant cedar. The Indians savoured*

166

*scarcely less of the luxuries, greatness and splendour of Cuzco in that distant, exiled land. And they enjoyed life there.'*

Then Francisco stretched himself out on the crumbled earth as if on a horizontal cross, and tried to induce his grief. He whispered a prayer of penitence, then a petition for forgiveness. At the same time he realised: this pain was inflicted on me, by me. The conquistadors are gone, the Inca are gone.

But the tears did not come. He felt only an indefinable self-despisal, like the aftertaste of a dish he had forgotten.

Kneeling at the rock's foot, he drew the quartzite mirror from its cloth, feeling how cold it was, how smooth and light, as if disburdened of all it had seen. He pulled a loose stone from the walls and thrust his hand into the hole. There was earth beyond: a nest of compost. He bowed his head.

Then he became aware of luxuriating in his act. He was watching his own humility. He was pious, wasn't he, and even beautiful: a young man with a priceless gift, surrendering it to where it belonged, redeeming his people? He felt an instant of despair. This self, this sin, comprised everything he was.

He did not look at himself in the disc. He would immure it without knowing if it still contained his reflection. It did not matter. Little about him mattered any more. A human being is not pure, he thought. Only God is pure. A human being, like his ancestors, is made of parts.

Then he closed his eyes and thrust the mirror into the hole. If God forgave him for desecrating the Eucharist, he would return to the seminary and become a priest. He would serve as a channel between God and His flock. He sealed the hole with the loose stone, and pushed some dust into its crevices. Even the local Indians would not find the mirror now. As he knelt under the boulder, clasping his hands, the plea whispered from his mouth: *'Have pity upon all those whom thou hast created . . .'*

He had forgotten that this was an Inca prayer.